**"I won't be married to you anymore!"
she said through tight lips.**

"Why not?" His hands gripped her loosely. Now that their bodies were so close, she was trapped by the memory of her own emotions. Even when Morgan felt most alienated from her, she had only to move into his arms and the flame of sexuality would flare between them.

She looked up at him through her long lashes. She felt her lips part in unspoken invitation. She forgot all the good reasons she had for keeping him at a safe distance.

"Morgan . . ." she said huskily, tracing the outline of his mouth with one tentative finger.

Dear Reader:

After more than one year of publication, SECOND CHANCE AT LOVE has a lot to celebrate. Not only has it become firmly established as a major line of paperback romances, but response from our readers also continues to be warm and enthusiastic. Your letters keep pouring in—and we love receiving them. We're getting to know you—your likes and dislikes—and want to assure you that your contribution does make a difference.

As we work hard to offer you better and better SECOND CHANCE AT LOVE romances, we're especially gratified to hear that you, the reader, are rating us higher and higher. After all, our success depends on *you*. We're pleased that you enjoy our books and that you appreciate the extra effort our writers and staff put into them. Thanks for spreading the good word about SECOND CHANCE AT LOVE and for giving us your loyal support. Please keep your suggestions and comments coming!

With warm wishes,

Ellen Edwards

Ellen Edwards
SECOND CHANCE AT LOVE
The Berkley/Jove Publishing Group
200 Madison Avenue
New York, NY 10016

Second Chance at Love

STORMY REUNION
JASMINE CRAIG

A
SECOND CHANCE AT LOVE
BOOK

STORMY REUNION

Copyright © 1982 by Jasmine Craig

Distributed by Berkley/Jove

First edition published October 1982

First printing

"Second Chance at Love" and the butterfly emblem are trademarks belonging to Jove Publications, Inc.

Printed in the United States of America

Second Chance at Love books are published by
The Berkley/Jove Publishing Group
200 Madison Avenue, New York, NY, 10016

STORMY REUNION

Chapter One

SHE SET THE BOWL of baby cereal in front of Andy and gave him his spoon with the picture of Big Bird on the handle. He clutched it tightly in his chubby fist and began to scoop up the oatmeal. He was proud of his skill at feeding himself, and his eyes soon screwed almost shut with the effort of concentration.

Brooke watched him for a moment, feeling a sudden irrational twist of love when a large dollop of oatmeal fell off the spoon and into his lap.

"Fall down," Andy pronounced, his blue eyes opening wide with astonishment. "All fall down," he added as he experimentally pushed another spoonful straight from the bowl onto his knees.

"Yes, I'm afraid it did all fall down." Brooke wiped the sticky spoon on a paper towel and handed it back to him. "You're doing so well eating by yourself, Andy. Try again."

She patted his blond hair affectionately and leaned

1

across him to flip the switch on the portable television. She might as well listen to the news and find out which group of terrorists had blown up what recently. It seemed days since she had last found time to buy and read a newspaper.

She slipped a couple of slices of bread into the toaster and yawned as the television newscaster announced another change in the government's economic forecast. It was at least a week since she had watched the morning news, but she was sure she'd heard the same things last time. She flipped channels. On one station somebody was interviewing a fashion designer who thought men ought to wear long skirts. So elegant, the designer was saying. The Chinese have been doing it for *years*. Brooke decided to watch the designer. On the whole, he was more interesting than yet another lecture on why the Federal Reserve Bank had goofed in estimating the national money supply.

She gave Andy his mug of apple juice and poured herself a cup of coffee, yawning again as a parade of male models twirled across the screen, displaying the new skirts for men. She was tired. She hadn't managed to leave work last night until almost two A.M., and Andy had awakened her this morning before seven. She cradled the cup in her hands, hoping the hot coffee would boost her energy level.

The designer faded from the screen, and a local Boston announcer began to read the news headlines. Brooke listened with less than half her attention. Suddenly her hands began to shake, and the coffee cup she was holding fell to the floor.

She didn't notice the scalding liquid soaking through her robe and spreading a brown stain over her lap. "No!" she said, instinctively shutting her eyes so that she would not have to watch the flickering images in front of her. Her hand reached out automatically to switch off the television, and she sat for a moment staring blankly at the empty gray screen. As soon as she realized what she had done, she pressed the button to turn the picture back on. It was too late. The television newscaster was reading the details of a revised pay scale for city firefighters.

She left the kitchen, not even aware that Andy had started to cry, and walked blindly across the cramped living room and out the front door. She knocked on the door of her apartment-house neighbor.

Joan Krakowski came to the door, her homely face breaking into a cheerful smile when she saw who was there. "Brooke, honey! What are you doing out and about so early in the morning?"

"Do you have a newspaper?" She was vaguely aware that Joan had spoken, but she had no idea what the woman had said.

"A newspaper? You mean this morning's?"

"Yes. Could I borrow it, please?"

Joan disappeared and came back a few moments later with the newspaper tucked under her arm. "You're lucky Joe didn't take it with him this morning."

Brooke accepted the paper without comment. Halfway across the narrow hall she stopped and swung round, remembering her neighbor's existence.

"Thank you for the paper," she said.

She reentered her apartment and sat at the kitchen table. She turned the pages of the paper feverishly, paying no attention to Andy's cries. He was unused to being ignored, and his sobs turned into a persistent, complaining wail.

She found the story on the first page of the financial section. The private plane carrying scientist Morgan Kent to a conference in California had crashed into a military proving ground on the Arizona/California border. Morgan Kent was founder and president of Kent Industries of Boston, the paper noted. Five other people had been on the plane, and there were no survivors.

No survivors. The words pounded inside her head so that the noise of them blotted out all other sounds. She jumped violently when she felt somebody touching her arm. She found Joan's worried face looming over her.

"Brooke, honey, are you all right? You were acting so strange just now, and then I could hear Andy crying. You look dreadful, honey. You're whiter than a ghost. Is there something I can do?"

Joan's words brought her back to some realization of the world around her. She became aware of the fact that Andy was howling at the top of his very powerful lungs. He had upended his cereal bowl over his head and then thrown it onto the floor, where it lay in the middle of the pool of coffee left by her dropped cup. Globules of oatmeal clung to his hair, and he was alternately banging his fist on the table and attempting to wipe grains of cereal from his eyes.

She jumped up and lifted Andy from his chair. His howling stopped, as if by magic, leaving the kitchen ominously silent. *No survivors.* The words started to pound in her head again, and she buried her face against the stickiness of Andy's cheeks, as if that way she could make the words go away.

Joan thrust her back into the chair. "Brooke, you're going to pass out if you're not careful. What is it? What's happened?"

Brooke cleared her throat, not quite sure if she would be able to speak. "It's my husband," she said, squeezing the words past the lump in her throat. Scrupulously, she corrected herself. "That is, I mean my ex-husband. He's dead." The words echoed round the kitchen and she looked up, her eyes glazed over with shock. "He's dead," she repeated.

It was the first time Brooke had ever told Joan about her husband.

"I'm sorry," Joan said. "Do you want me to look after

Andy for a while? I guess you might like a few hours to yourself."

"You're very kind, but I'll be all right." Suddenly the tears started to trickle out of her eyes, and once they started to fall she couldn't stop them. She turned away because she hated anybody, even Joan, to see her grief. She grabbed a couple of tissues and scrubbed at her damp cheeks. It isn't grief, she told herself fiercely. My God, you can't be crazy enough to mourn Morgan Kent. You're not that much of a masochist.

She forced herself to turn around and face her neighbor.

"I didn't know you were married." Joan's words broke the tense silence of the kitchen and were left hanging in the air between them.

"I'm not married anymore," Brooke said at last. "I haven't seen Morgan for nearly two years. It makes no difference to anything. . . . It was just the shock of hearing it on television. He was always so alive." So arrogantly alive, she thought. So damn sure of himself and his rightful place in the universe.

Joan took Andy from Brooke's arms. "I'll bathe him," she said. "I'll get the cereal out of his hair. I'll do it in my apartment because the twins are both in the playpen and I can't leave them any longer." Joan had two-year-old twin girls in addition to a six-month-old baby boy.

"Thank you." Brooke spoke politely, although she'd only half-heard what had been said to her. Joan carried Andy to the front door, then turned with a puzzled, half-guilty look on her face.

"How come they announced your husband's death on the news . . . and put it in the paper and all?"

"He's the head of the largest computer-chip manufacturing company in the Boston area," Brooke said. "I mean, he *was* the head."

"He was a pretty important guy, I guess."

"Yes."

Joan shifted Andy to her other hip, and Brooke could imagine her wondering why the ex-wife of such an influential man was living in a two-room walk-up in one of Boston's poorer neighborhoods. "Come and get Andy when you're ready," was all Joan said. "I'm not going out until lunch time. Takes me until then to clean the apartment. I swear those twins can wreck a room faster than any pair of kids I ever met."

Joan left and Brooke stood in the tiny kitchen, trying to think of what she could do next. She seemed to be frozen in a limbo where all decisions and all actions were equally impossible. Her foot knocked against the fallen coffee cup and she picked it up, noticing for the first time that the floor was covered with a disgusting mess of congealed cereal, apple juice, and spilled coffee.

She spent an hour cleaning the kitchen, scrubbing the counters and the floor so that the shabby surfaces gleamed with unaccustomed brilliance. She was glad of the work and regretful when it was finished. She knew it was important to leave herself no time to think. She wasn't ready to face up to any memories. Not today. Perhaps not ever.

She hurried out of the kitchen and, finding herself standing in the middle of the bedroom, made her bed and smoothed the covers in Andy's crib. She dusted some furniture, although it wasn't very dirty, but soon there was nothing left to do.

There *must* be something else. Usually the days seemed too short to complete all the tasks she needed to cram into them. She caught sight of her reflection in the mirror and saw she was wearing the coffee-stained robe, so she stripped it off and took a shower. She made the water as hot as she could bear and shampooed her long chestnut hair for good measure.

At some deep level of her subconscious she was aware of what she was doing, aware that she was trying to protect her raw, agonized feelings by hiding behind a barrier of trivial chores. The pretense worked to a certain extent. Despite everything, she was managing not to remember Morgan.

When she was dressed she hurried across the hall to Joan's apartment, anxious to be with Andy again. She would take him to the park. That way there would be no time to think. Ever since Andy had discovered the joys of running, he had relished putting his skill into constant practice. If she were chasing an active toddler around the playground, her mind would have no empty silences to fill.

Andy was playing with the twins, waiting for them to build him a tower of blocks, which he knocked down when he considered they had built a monument worthy of his attention. His cherubic face was scrubbed clean, and his hair shone so that threads of silver seemed to be woven into the soft, straw-colored thatch.

"Thank you, Joan, you've worked miracles," Brooke said.

"It was my pleasure. He's a cute kid, otherwise I wouldn't want to sit for him at night. I used to sit for Mrs. McConnell's kid, and believe me, for three dollars an hour it wasn't worth it."

"Andy's usually pretty good-tempered," Brooke agreed. She grabbed her son just before he could knock over another wobbly tower of blocks. "Come on, Andy, we have to get you dressed. Thanks again for cleaning him up."

"Will you be going to work tonight?" Joan asked.

"Yes." Brooke's answer was firm. "I need the money. Tony doesn't pay unless you do the work. I'll drop Andy off at the usual time if I may."

"See you at five-thirty then."

Brooke dressed Andy in corduroy coveralls and a warm woolen sweater. It was a sunny day, but in early October the wind often threatened a sudden chill. She got out his stroller, and he climbed in willingly, apparently pleased at the prospect of an outing so early in the day. She pushed him through the shabby streets near their apartment, in the direction of his favorite playground. The park was located in a more prosperous neighborhood than their own, and it was quite a distance to walk, but Andy seemed happily occupied watching the passing traffic.

Every so often a heavy truck would roar past, and Andy would observe its smoky exhaust with round-eyed pleasure.

"Truck," he would announce as it went by. "Big truck." If Brooke did not respond at once, he would repeat more loudly, "Mama look truck!"

He was good at conveying his wishes despite the limits of his vocabulary. He was probably genetically programmed to give commands, Brooke thought. It was a skill he apparently had inherited from his father.

The sudden image of Morgan Kent, his body crumpled in the searing heat of the Arizona desert, flashed into her mind and would not go away. She clenched the handles of Andy's stroller so tightly that her knuckles gleamed white with the strain. She had spent the last two years telling herself that she never wanted to see or hear of Morgan Kent again. But the knowledge that her wish had now come irreversibly true caused her no pleasure. She could feel the bar of grief tightening across her chest so that she could scarcely breathe. Morgan had never understood her, and now he never would. Their misunderstandings, the bitter accusations and counteraccusations, didn't matter anymore. The gap between them had widened into an unbridgeable abyss, and Brooke felt none of the relief she might have expected.

"Pretty. Nice." Andy's voice interrupted her painful thoughts, and Brooke realized she had been standing outside a florist's window for at least five minutes. On an impulse she didn't fully understand and didn't want to analyze she entered the store.

"Can I help you?" asked a young woman dressed in jeans and a smock. She was working an a small arrangement of fall flowers, twisting brown and gold chrysanthemums into a brilliant oval of color.

Brooke hesitated only for a moment. "I would like to send an arrangement similar to the one you're making to a town in New Hampshire. It's for . . . it's for a funeral. Could you send it today?"

"Yes, of course. If you'll just give me the details, the address and so on, I'll phone the order through right away. I expect the store there will be able to deliver the flowers this afternoon. Which town is it?"

"Rendford, New Hampshire. The address is Kent House, Kent Lane, Rendford."

The woman wrote down the details. "I could ask them to send a proper wreath if you would prefer it. This sort of arrangement isn't really what most people choose for a funeral," she said, faintly embarrassed. "As a matter of fact, this is a bridal bouquet for a wedding this afternoon."

"I don't want a wreath!" Brooke's voice was unexpectedly sharp. She drew a deep breath, softening her next words. "I'd like to send that arrangement, please, even though it's not traditional."

"Is there some special message to include with the card? And should we address it to any member of the family in particular?"

Her stomach twisted in a spasm of acute physical pain. "Just say: *For Morgan from Brooke. In memory.*" She felt the pain in her stomach churn into sickness, and she thrust a credit card into the young woman's hand. "Here," she said. "Could you make out the bill as quickly as possible, please?"

"Go walk," Andy announced loudly, wriggling against the straps that held him in the stroller. "Go walk." He was apparently tired of examining the flowers he had once thought pretty. Searching for a few more words to express his impatience, he ordered, "Get out! Go away!"

"We'll go in a minute," Brooke reassured him. She took the credit card back from the woman.

"I'll make sure the flowers get there today," the woman said.

"Thank you." Brooke hurried out of the shop before Andy's squirming body and flailing hands could knock anything over. With considerable effort she concentrated on her child. "Look, Andy!" she said, pointing to the road ahead of them. "There's a truck coming."

Andy watched the truck in a deeply satisfied silence. "Big truck," he said after the final set of wheels had roared past. "Big big truck."

They arrived at the entrance to the park, and Brooke lifted him out of his stroller with relief. "Let's play catch, Andy," she said. As they tossed the ball onto the grass, the cold misery of her loss lessened until it was no more than a tight knot of sadness coiled in her stomach . . . waiting for the moment when she would find herself alone.

Chapter Two

BROOKE STRUGGLED to produce a smile for the two new customers, even though it was after one in the morning and she suspected they were already three-fourths drunk.

"Welcome to Tony's nightclub," she said politely. Tony insisted that his employees be polite. "I run a classy establishment here," he frequently reminded them. "When you work for me, you gotta think class."

"Looks like a real nice place," one of the men said. "And we're sure ready to be entertained, hon."

Brooke hid her weariness behind another smile. Thirty-nine hours had passed since she had heard the news about Morgan, but her heartache seemed to have increased rather than diminished.

"Follow me, please, gentlemen," she said, pushing thoughts of Morgan aside. She started to weave her way expertly through the packed bar. Her head ached from the cigarette smoke and the constant blare of pop music, but tonight she was glad of the noise, glad of the cheerful

11

garishness of the nightclub where she worked. Senior hostess at Tony's Bar. Not exactly the career she'd once imagined for herself, but she was becoming quite proficient at her job. "You got the real thing," Tony had said when he'd promoted her the previous month. "You got class."

"We want a table up close to the show," the customer said, giving her a knowing wink. "We heard it's a good one, hon, so make sure our table's real close to the action." The man fumbled in his hip pocket and pulled out a crumpled bill. "Here, hon, tuck this in *your* hip pocket!" He nudged his friend, and together they gave a shout of laughter as they leered at the skin-tight satin of Brooke's backless dress.

She gritted her teeth and didn't speak until her voice was completely under control. "Thank you, sir," she said, accepting the tip. "Follow me, please."

"Willingly, sugar. You're a cute act to follow!" The men thumped each other on the back in drunken good humor. "Sure ain't any hardship to follow that pair of legs!"

Brooke looked down at the five-dollar bill clenched in her fist. For an insane moment she wondered what would happen if she turned around and shoved the bill straight into the man's wide-open mouth. But sanity prevailed, and she crushed the bill more tightly in her hand. She needed the money, and it was a bit late to start worrying about her personal dignity. She wondered what Morgan would say if he could see her now. He would no doubt consider her present job proof of all his darkest suspicions. Did dead people have suspicions? She forced the pointless questions out of her mind. Don't think about the past, she reminded herself. Just worry about the present and how you're going to pay for Andy's winter clothes.

She found the men a couple of empty seats close to

the tiny stage and wended her way back to the club's main entrance. Tony put his arm out to stop her passage.

"You okay, Brooke? You look like hell."

"Thanks." Her mouth twisted into a wry smile. "Is that your new line in flattery, Tony? If so, I don't think much of it."

He looked away from her, staring at a swirling strobe light. "I heard about Morgan Kent's plane," he said brusquely. "Sure was a hell of a way to go."

Her violet eyes dilated with shock. "How did you know? Who told you about Morgan . . . and me?"

He turned back to face her, and his eyes were kind as they looked at her, momentarily softening the cynical cast of his features. "Hey, kid, in my business it pays to keep informed. I know the right people to ask for information. But don't worry. I never told nobody."

She tried to recover her poise, forcing her feelings back behind their usual calm mask. "There's nothing for you to tell, anyway. Morgan and I were married for less than a year, and it was all over between us more than two years ago."

"If you say so." The golden medallions dangling at the open neck of his purple shirt glinted as he turned away. "There's a guy at the door, kid. Go get him."

She was glad to have an excuse to continue across the crowded floor, away from Tony's too perceptive gaze. She could see the man, tall and dressed in a dark suit, waiting by the velvet rope barrier. People often came to Tony's alone, and as far as she could judge in the dim light, he was completely sober. Smoothing her long hair with a tired gesture, Brooke fixed a smile on her face and moved forward to greet the new arrival. At least if he was sober he was unlikely to cause any trouble.

"Good evening, sir. Welcome to Tony's."

He turned at the sound of her voice, and she saw him clearly for the first time. She felt the blood drain from her cheeks, leaving her skin ghostly white under its makeup.

He hasn't changed a bit, she thought wildly. He's still the same arrogant bastard.

His features were every bit as hard as she remembered, and his gray eyes glittered coldly as they assessed her appearance. His mouth was clamped tightly shut, but she remembered—oh God, how she remembered!—the betraying sensuality of his lower lip. The red overhead light cast a fiery ring around the silver thickness of his hair, but his eyes weren't even fractionally warmed by the glow of the lamp.

"Hello, Brooke," he said softly, and she shivered as she heard the familiar, clipped accent.

She moistened her lips with the tip of her tongue, swallowing the sickening lump of terror in her throat. "No...," she said. "You're dead. Can't you leave me in peace even when you're dead?" For one moment she felt a surge of insane, overwhelming joy, then some instinct of self-preservation took over and she jerked away from him, getting ready to run.

His hand whipped out, gripping her by the wrist. "I'll take you to your apartment," he said quietly. "We have things to talk about."

"No!" she exclaimed again. "You can't force me!" The anguished protest escaped before she could cut it off. She hadn't meant to sound so helpless. There were more than 226 million people in the United States, but for two years she had lived in dread of the day he would find her. How ironic that it should be his presumed death that brought her out of hiding, blowing away the security of the new life she had tried to build. "Take your hands off me," she said, her voice low. "We have *nothing* to say to each other. We said it all two years ago."

"No, we didn't. You ran away before we could discuss anything."

She drew in her breath on an incredulous, shaky laugh. *"Ran away!"* she exclaimed. "Is that the story you handed out to your friends and relations? That *I* ran away?"

"It's the truth," he said quietly.

"I always knew you were a bastard, Morgan. I didn't know you were a liar as well."

Tony arrived in the lobby. He had an infallible instinct for potential trouble. "Everything okay here, darling?" he asked her, his clever, world-weary eyes assessing Morgan with unconcealed interest.

"I'm Morgan Kent." Morgan spoke before Brooke could gather her scattered wits. "I'm going to take my wife home, if you don't mind. She's had rather a shock."

"Good to meet you, Mr. Kent." Tony shook Morgan's hand enthusiastically. Brooke knew he always enjoyed meeting a celebrity, and enjoyed boasting of it afterward even more. "I guess you weren't killed in that plane crash after all."

"No, I wasn't killed," Morgan agreed dryly.

"That was some mistake the media made. How come? Are those reporters so dumb they can't tell a dead body from a live man?"

Morgan didn't answer immediately, and Brooke thought he would refuse to reply. After a short pause he lifted his shoulders in an infinitesimal shrug, but his eyes seemed to study her with a curious intensity. "I had a speaking engagement in San Diego," he said finally. "At the last minute I found I couldn't go and I asked my brother to take my place. Unfortunately my name must have remained on the plane's list of passengers. It was a company plane and I guess nobody bothered to make the change."

"Your b-brother took your place on the plane?" Brooke stammered. "You mean *Andrew* was killed in the crash?"

"Yes."

Her face had been pale before. Now it turned gray. She couldn't meet the hard anger in Morgan's eyes, so she looked at Tony instead, clutching his arm in an instinctive appeal for support. He pushed her onto the lobby's only chair, but it was too late. The edge of his features started to blur, and she had to bend her head to her knees in order to avoid the dizziness that threatened her.

She was not granted the respite of even a few moments of unconsciousness. The dizziness passed far too quickly. Tony was all solicitude, clucking like a mother hen as he escorted her out of the lobby and into his office. He left as soon as she was settled into his leather chair, murmuring a few words to Morgan as he closed the office door.

Brooke steeled herself to look up and meet Morgan's furious gaze. She knew exactly why he was so angry.

"Drink this," he ordered curtly, holding out a glass of water.

She sipped it obediently, because that way she didn't have to speak. Of course he had misinterpreted the reason for her shock. He couldn't be expected to understand the strange mixture of fear, despair, and relief that she had felt on hearing of Andrew's death.

"Two years!" Morgan said. The words seemed to spill out against his will. "You haven't seen him for two years, but you almost fainted when you heard he was dead. My God, Brooke, if you loved him that much, why didn't you marry him?"

She wasn't prepared to tell Morgan the truth. She wasn't going to give him an opportunity to tear apart the fragile harmony of her life with Andy. "He didn't want to marry me," she lied. She managed to push her hair out of her eyes with a defiant gesture, although the room was starting to spin round her once again. "You know what your brother was like," she said. "He needed a fresh face on the pillow next to him every couple of months."

Morgan turned from her with a low exclamation of contempt. He made no other comment on her statement. "Tony has gone to fetch your coat so that I can take you home," he said.

She was icy cold and so nauseated that it was difficult to think. But it didn't require any thought at all to know that she couldn't bear to go home with him. He would invade the sanctuary of her apartment, filling every inch of it with memories of his presence, torturing her with reminders of how they once had felt for each other.

"I don't want you to take me home," she whispered.

Morgan's face darkened with anger. "Why did you send me those flowers, Brooke?"

"I don't know." She took refuge in a deliberate blankness of mind, although she was careful not to meet Morgan's eyes, which she knew would detect traces of the emotions she wanted to conceal. Why had she allowed herself to relax those carefully erected mental shields? Why had she allowed herself to remember how much she once had loved him?

He wasn't satisfied with her evasion, and he walked over to her side, capturing her pale face between his hands and forcing her to look up at him.

"Why did you send the flowers, Brooke?"

She trembled at the familiar touch of his hands on her skin, then lowered her lashes to screen the turmoil in her eyes. She wanted to deny him the satisfaction of a reply, but the words seemed to be dragged out of her. "Because once, a long time ago, I loved you. Because . . . for a little while . . . we were very happy."

She was surprised to hear the sudden exhalation of his breath, as if her answer had been important to him and he hadn't known what she would say. "I've often wondered if my memories of those first few weeks were just an illusion," he said harshly. "I'm flattered to discover that even you seem to think we once shared something special." His hands relaxed their grip, and she pulled herself away from him. She didn't want him to guess how profoundly his nearness still affected her.

"I'm afraid I don't have time to rake over stale memories, Morgan. I have to get back to work." She spoke sharply to hide the turmoil of her feelings. "Tony may look as though he's all heart, but actually he only pays for services rendered."

For a moment she was frightened by the rage her words provoked, but Tony came into the office just as she finished speaking. The violence in Morgan's face was immediately smoothed away, leaving his expression polite and impersonal.

"Brooke, you look worse than ever. Worse than last night." Tony's voice cut across her chaotic thoughts. "Go home with Mr. Kent, Brooke. Ginny can cover for you at the door. Get some rest or you'll make yourself sick. I can tell you didn't sleep a wink last night."

She didn't have the mental energy to fight both of them, and in any case she wasn't sure she would be capable of working anymore tonight. She felt so chilled that she wondered if she would ever be completely warm again. With the tiny, rational part of her brain that was still functioning, she realized that she was in shock and not wholly answerable for her actions. Most of her mind, however, was too numb to think anything at all, and she stood docilely while Tony fastened the buttons of her coat.

"I'll call you a cab," he offered.

"I have my car outside, thank you," Morgan replied.

She gave a quick, breathless laugh. "Of course you do."

Tony glanced at her, surprised by the edge of hysteria

in her words. How could she explain to him that Morgan Kent was the sort of man who always had a car waiting to speed him to his destination? Other people might get bogged down in the trivial details of their lives, but Morgan knew just where he was going and was able to overcome problems that would have defeated a more fallible human being. Brooke had personally experienced the way he dealt with problems. She had turned out to be one, so he had cut her out of his life with single-minded ruthlessness.

"Let's go, Brooke," he said. She followed him outside, keeping her face absolutely blank so that he wouldn't see how she felt when his arm reached out to support her shaky steps.

"See you tomorrow, Tony," she said and marveled at the note of cheerfulness she managed to inject into her voice.

A silver-gray Cadillac Cimarron stood in the no-parking zone outside the nightclub, and a chauffeur sprang out from his seat behind the wheel as soon as they approached. Morgan pulled a couple of bills from his wallet and handed them to the driver. "Take a cab back to Rendford, Ed. I'm going to drive myself tonight."

"Yes, sir."

"Let my people at the office know that I'll be out of reach until tomorrow afternoon."

"Yes, Mr. Kent." The chauffeur was well trained. Not a muscle moved in his face as he received the instructions. His eyes carefully avoided Brooke. He cleared his throat.

"Your father . . . er, is there some message for your father, Mr. Kent?"

"I'll stop by tomorrow and see him before I go to the office."

"Yes, sir." The chauffeur made no further comment. He held the door open for Brooke while Morgan slid behind the steering wheel, then he faded rapidly and discreetly into the darkness.

Morgan put the car into gear and drove off without asking Brooke for directions. "How do you know where I live?" she asked.

"A private investigator traced you through the flowers you sent. You paid by credit card, so the florist had a record both of the name you're using now and of your address. I already went to your apartment house, and a woman there told me you were at work. That's why I went to the club."

"I see." She had guessed as much even before he answered her. "I should have known you'd find me. The flowers were the only mistake I made in two years, but it was all you needed, wasn't it, Morgan?"

"I've been trying to find you ever since you left Rendford," he said evenly, astonishing Brooke by the admission. His profile looked grim in the flickering headlights of a passing car. "Why were you so anxious to hide, for God's sake? What were you afraid of? You changed your name to Erickson. You didn't draw on any of your bank accounts. You never made contact with any of your old college friends. You never even wrote to my brother."

"I wanted to get away from the Kent family."

"I suppose it never occurred to you that people might be worried about your safety?"

"No," she replied. "That never occurred to me. I did leave you a note."

He swore softly under his breath, then fell silent. Brooke stared out the window at the deserted, darkened streets. The car seemed full of an unwelcome tension stretching ever tighter between the two of them, and she could think of no way to control it.

"I heard your grandmother died," Morgan said suddenly. "I was very sorry."

"Yes, she died about three months before my ba...after

I left Rendford. It was a terrible blow." The brief words hid a great deal of grief. When her grandmother died, Brooke was six months pregnant. There had been moments in the following weeks when she had wondered if she could possibly make it through her pregnancy alone. Only a stubborn pride and the knowledge that she could never again live in the shadow of Morgan's suspicions had enabled her to survive the lonely ordeal of Andy's birth. If she had known her grandmother would die, she might never have summoned up the courage to leave Rendford, despite Morgan's threats.

"How did you know?" she asked. "That my grandmother died, I mean."

"Private investigators, again," he said. "Despite what you wrote in your note, it took me a couple of weeks to realize you'd run away for good. I was sure you'd go to your grandmother's, but by the time I tried to contact you, she'd moved. It took the detective agency four months to trace where she'd gone. Eventually we found her new address in Boston, but by then she was dead and you'd moved away. I didn't know where to look next. I even tried to trace you through your father."

Against her will her head jerked up. "You managed to contact my father? You *have* been keeping your detective agency busy."

Morgan avoided her eyes. "Your father had taken out a new marriage license. Did you know he was married again?"

"Oh, yes, I knew," Brooke said. "He sent my grandmother and me a postcard when he and his fourth wife were on their honeymoon. Of course he didn't bother to give us his return address. I suppose he considered that too risky. One of us might have asked him for some help."

"He's an unhappy man, Brooke. He's never really recovered from your mother's death."

"Oh, sure! I suppose he told you he's spent the past fifteen years avoiding the sight of me because I remind him of his dead true love! If he loved my mother so passionately, how come he's managed to find three other women he's willing to put in her place? Not to mention the little matter of abandoning me to my grandmother's care?"

"He hasn't found three other woman to replace your mother," Morgan said quietly. "That's precisely the problem."

When Brooke refused to reply, Morgan changed the subject. "Your father was a whole lot easier to find than you were," he said. "I assumed you would go as far away from Rendford as you possibly could. We searched for you in California and Texas and half the other states in the country. It never occurred to us to look right under our noses in Boston."

"You didn't think I'd have the temerity to live so close to the lion's den? Is that what you mean?"

"No," he said, with a harsh intake of breath. "That isn't what I meant and you know it."

She could tell he was uncomfortable, and she was strangely elated by the knowledge. "What is it, Morgan?" she taunted. "Are you angry because one of your victims had the courage to escape?"

"You're so sure you were the victim in our marriage, aren't you, Brooke?"

"Yes," she said tersely. "I was definitely the victim. You and Andrew did your best to ruin my life."

He pulled the car over to the curb in a violent swerve, stepping hard on the brakes. "I believe this is your apartment building," he said.

He opened the car door for her and she got out, taking care not to touch him. They walked across the littered sidewalk in silence. For the first time, she forced herself to see the neighborhood through Morgan's eyes. The people living on this street were poor, and the buildings reflected their owners' lack of cash. The paint peeled from the doors and windows, and the tiny yards grew nothing except untidy brown grass. Half a dozen empty beer cans rattled in the gutters, stirred by a gust of autumn wind.

She refused to apologize for where she lived. It was a financial struggle to support herself and Andy, but she did it. She wasn't in debt, and she was proud of her accomplishment in providing for her child. She inserted her key in the apartment building's outer door and walked along the dingy corridor to her apartment. She wouldn't allow herself to look round to observe Morgan's reaction.

She unlocked her front door and gestured to him to precede her into the living room. "What do you want to talk about, Morgan?" she asked as calmly as she could. "I'm sure you'll appreciate that it's been a rough day and I want to get some sleep."

He didn't answer, but walked around the living room examining the cheap, secondhand furniture without commenting. She had done her best to brighten up the room with white paint and colorful cushions, but she could not deny that in comparison to Kent House this apartment was almost a hovel. Morgan didn't stop his restless inspection until his foot knocked against a cardboard carton stuffed with a child's plastic building blocks. He glanced up and his gaze fell on a framed picture of Andy.

He picked up the photograph, his face wiped utterly clean of expression. "Is this...your baby?" he asked, and only the harshness of his voice betrayed the raw emotion he was holding in check.

"Yes." Her mouth was so dry it was hard to get even the single syllable out clearly.

"I gave you the money to have an abortion. I gave you cash. It was the only thing you took from the house. I assumed you had used it."

"I did use it. I needed the money to support myself for the first two months after he...my baby...was born."

"He?"

"I have a son."

Morgan looked down at the picture, a grim smile twisting his mouth. "He looks like a handsome little boy. No doubt he takes after his father." Tension again filled the silence stretching between them, but she was determined not to speak. "What's his name?" he asked at last.

She raised her chin, knowing he would misunderstand, but a sudden burst of the sort of false pride that had caused her problems in the first place overtook her. "I call him Andy," she said defiantly. "But the name on his birth certificate is Andrew Kent."

"Of course! What else?" He slammed the picture face down on the table. "Well, I guess I should be grateful you were honest when you named him, even if you refused to tell me the truth."

"Is that why you came all this way, Morgan? So that you could insult me some more? Didn't you have your fill of that while we were married?"

"I seem to remember that the insults weren't all one-sided." The line of his mouth tightened a fraction more, but his voice was once again colorless as he continued speaking. "I didn't intend to start an argument, Brooke. I hoped to discuss this with you in a civilized fashion, but it seems that conventional politeness is impossible between us."

Suddenly she was unutterably weary. "Perhaps you're right, Morgan. It's three o'clock in the morning, and I need some sleep. Could you say whatever it is you came to say and then get out?"

Color darkened the tan of his cheeks. "I came here at the request of the family lawyers," he said, and only the faint flicker of a muscle in his jaw betrayed the strain he was feeling. "I've come to inform you of a bequest under the terms of my brother's will."

"Bequest?" Her legs began to shake with apprehension, and she sat down hastily in the nearest chair.

"Apart from some donations to charity, Andrew left almost everything he possessed to you."

Brooke pressed her hand against her mouth, smothering a hysterical sob of half-tears, half-laughter. She fought to control her convulsive gasps for breath. Oh, Andrew! she thought. Even when you're dead your good intentions cause me nothing but trouble.

Morgan muttered an angry expletive, and the sound of his voice effectively silenced her sobs. She looked up at him, keeping her face blank.

"What were the terms of Andrew's will?" she asked.

"My brother owned eight percent of the stock in Kent Industries," Morgan told her in the same expressionless voice he had used before. "At today's market price that makes you a very wealthy woman."

"How frustrating for you!" Blind rage at Morgan chased away the lingering remnants of her hysteria. "I'm sure you feel that a life of endless poverty would be more appropriate for a sinful woman like me!"

"The lawyers need you to come with me to New Hampshire," he said, ignoring her outburst. "There are a great many matters they have to discuss with you."

She felt panic start to swell, threatening to burst out of her. Morgan would see it and know the effect he had upon her still. "I'm not going back to Kent House! The lawyers can write to me."

"For God's sake, Brooke! We're not talking about a simple hundred-dollar legacy. We're talking about eight percent of the voting shares in a successful company. *My* company."

The hurts and pains that she thought had been buried for nearly two years started to throb in an unceasing rhythm. "I'm not coming," she repeated stubbornly, not attempting to justify her position. Perhaps if she said the words often enough they might come true. "There's Andy to think of," she said with sudden inspiration. "I can't leave Andy."

There was a pause. "Of course I realize you have to bring . . . the child . . . with you," Morgan said.

Just for a moment she was tempted to take him up on his reluctant offer. She was seized with a longing she could hardly explain to introduce Andy to his heritage, to make him known to his grandfather. The madness passed quickly. "I would never subject my son to that sort of humiliation," she said. "Do you think he's too young to sense when people dislike him? You can't even bring yourself to say his name! Do you think I'm going to take Andy to New Hampshire, knowing how he would be treated by your family once we arrived there?"

She had won her point, as she had known she would. Even Morgan couldn't want to face the prospect of introducing Andy to his family. She wondered why her victory tasted so bitter and turned away to avoid looking into Morgan's suddenly bleak expression.

"Go away, Morgan," she said. "Go back to New Hampshire and tell the lawyers to call me. I promise to answer the phone."

He said nothing, and finally she heard the sound of his agile footsteps moving across the tiny living room. "We're both exhausted," he said. "It's better if I leave you for now. Good night, Brooke. We'll talk again in the morning."

She turned round swiftly to tell him that they had nothing more to talk about, but he was closer than she had thought and she almost fell against his body. She heard the sudden rush of an indrawn breath and realized that it was her own. For an endless moment they stared at one another. Brooke tried to drag her gaze away from the lean face that loomed over hers, but she was incapable of moving. All she could think about was the sudden tightness of her throat and the feel of Morgan's hands on her bare shoulders. She swayed toward him involuntarily, and for a moment his eyes darkened with unmistakable desire. Her lips parted in an instinctive gesture, and he thrust her away from him.

"Oh God, no! Not that!" he breathed. "You're not going to trap me that way again."

Brooke's voice seemed as frozen as her emotions. "Get out, Morgan," she said. "And don't come back ever again."

He didn't answer. She closed her eyes, unable to bear the sight of his self-contempt . After an eternity of time she heard the front door slam shut.

She stood without moving just where he had left her, staring unseeingly across the room. "Andy," she murmured after several moments of silent inactivity. "I must get Andy."

She let herself into Joan's apartment with her own key and lifted Andy from the portable crib that was erected each night in the Krakowski's living room. Andy stirred, but Brooke knew he wasn't really awakened by the familiar nightly ritual. His fist swung out, accidentally knocking her chin, and he smiled sleepily. "Night Momma," he said.

She buried her face in the soft warmth of his bundled body. "Good night, Andy," she whispered. "I love you."

He half-opened his eyes and patted his plump fingers against her cheek. "Pretty," he said. "Good night."

Chapter Three

At precisely eight o'clock in the morning Brooke heard the doorbell ring indicating that somebody was at the outer door of her apartment building. She did her best to ignore the persistent buzz. Perhaps he'll go away, she thought, certain that Morgan was at the door.

After three long rings the noise stopped abruptly, and she let out her breath in a sigh of relief. Seeing that her fists were clenched into two tight balls, she deliberately relaxed them. It couldn't have been Morgan, she thought. He'd never have given up so easily.

She felt as though she had been granted a reprieve from some dreadful ordeal. She had no doubt, though, that Morgan would try to see her again, and she was seized by an urgent need to escape from her apartment before he arrived. Her feelings had been in tumult ever since she'd heard of Morgan's supposed death, and emotions she would rather have kept hidden still hovered dangerously close to the surface. She knew she would have to be in better control of herself before risking another encounter with him.

"Come on, Andy," she said, pulling him out of his highchair. "We have to go to the store and buy ice cream."

Andy smiled, pushing aside the last of his breakfast. Any trip outside the apartment building met with his approval, and a trip to the supermarket was almost as much fun as a trip to the park.

He was quiet and cooperative while Brooke wiped his sticky face and fingers, and he did his best to help her when she started to dress him in warm clothes. He thrust his hand through the narrow opening in his sweater sleeve, crowing triumphantly when the same hand emerged mysteriously from the long knitted tube.

"Clever boy, Andy," Brooke said, but for once her attention was far removed from her son. She sat him on the edge of her bed and hastily tied the laces of his sturdy white walking shoes. The insteps were becoming a little tight, she noticed, and for a moment she worried about the need to buy yet another pair of good-quality leather shoes. Then she remembered. She was rich, an heiress. She never needed to worry about money again.

She started to laugh, then clamped her lips tightly shut to silence the high-pitched sound. She was well aware of the fact that she had been teetering on the brink of hysteria for the past two days. The fact that she was critically short of sleep didn't help to stabilize her mood.

She heard a knock at the front door, and her hands tightened so convulsively around Andy that he gave a squeal of protest. "Sorry, baby," she said, pressing a quick kiss against his cheek.

She held out her hand and Andy clasped it, trotting alongside her to the front door. At eighteen months old he was perfectly stable on his feet, but he had to move his legs quickly to keep up with her.

"Who is it?" she called out when she reached the bolted front door.

"It's me, Joan."

Brooke's body sagged with relief. Idiot, she scolded herself. You're becoming paranoid about Morgan. Quickly she pulled back the bolts, ready to smile a greeting at her friend.

The welcome died out of her eyes as soon as she saw who was waiting in the hall. In a reflex action she tried to slam the door shut, but Morgan guessed her intention and thrust his body into the opening.

She gave up the unequal struggle to keep him out of her home and collapsed against the wall, the final remnant of color draining from her cheeks. She couldn't manage to say anything, and Joan hurried into the living room behind Morgan, holding out her hands toward Brooke.

Andy ignored Joan's familiar presence and stared with silent interest at the tall, grey-eyed stranger.

Joan stared at the gray shadows beneath Brooke's eyes.

"Hey, have I done the wrong thing, hon?" she questioned her friend anxiously. "Mr. Kent told me that he needed to see you about some important family business, and he said you weren't answering your buzzer. I knew you were in here, so I let him in. I hope I didn't do wrong?"

"No. What you did was fine." Brooke pushed her long hair out of her eyes and forced herself to meet Joan's worried gaze with a smile. Her friend had merely been trying to help, and there was no point in blaming other people for Morgan's reappearance in her life. She alone was responsible for that. One way or another he would have found her once she made the mistake of sending those flowers.

"Morgan's right," she said. "We do have a couple of

things to discuss. It was just a shock seeing him there. That's why I tried to shut the door. I guess I'm tired and not thinking too straight."

"Don't worry, Mrs. Krakowski, I'll take good care of Brooke. I can see that she needs some time to recover from the shocks of the past few days." Morgan's voice had its usual charming edge, and Brooke could see Joan melting visibly under its impact.

"Well, I'm glad I did the right thing." Joan smiled a little uncertainly at both of them and stepped back out into the dingy apartment corridor. "I'll be right across the way if you need me for anything, Brooke. Stop over for a cup of coffee before you go to work tonight."

"I'll do that. Thanks, Joan."

Brooke waited in rigid silence until Joan disappeared behind her apartment door, then she turned to Morgan.

"I suppose you may as well come in and sit down, since I'm not strong enough to lock you out."

Andy must have sensed some of her resentment, for he hurried up to her and tugged anxiously at her hand. "Momma?" he questioned, and the doubt in his voice forced Brooke to pull herself together. She bent down and gathered him into her arms, smoothing his hair in an unconscious gesture of reassurance. "It's all right, Andy," she said. "Mommy will take you for a walk soon."

She carried him into the center of the living room and sat down in one of the shabby vinyl-covered armchairs, removing the stuffed frog that Andy always pushed behind the cushions. She kept her son on her lap, glad of the heavy, secure warmth of his body.

Morgan sat down opposite her. He looked exhausted, she thought as she made a quick, involuntary appraisal of his features. But then why shouldn't he? The last three days couldn't have been easy for him. He must have gone to find her immediately after his brother's funeral.

Why such desperate haste? she wondered. She accidentally caught his eyes and deliberately turned her gaze
away. She didn't want to feel sympathy for Morgan Kent.
She didn't want to feel *anything*.

"This is . . . Andy . . . of course." His voice interrupted
her chaotic thoughts and she nodded, not trusting herself
to speak.

"He looks very . . . robust," Morgan said slowly.

For a moment anger replaced her numb feelings.
"Aren't you going to say hello to him, Morgan? He's a
person, you know. He can talk."

With evident hesitation Morgan approached their
chair. He squatted down so that his face was more or
less on a level with Andy's. He cleared his throat, and
Brooke reflected that she had never before seen him so
unsure of himself. "Er . . . hello, Andy," he said finally.
"How are you this morning?"

Andy's gray eyes appraised Morgan with nerverack-
ing and silent thoroughness, then his face split into a
grin. "Dadda," he said. "Dadda come walk."

A moment of stunned silence enveloped the tiny living
room, and Morgan's face slowly stained with a wash of
dark color. For a moment Brooke didn't know where to
look. Whatever she had expected Andy to say, it certainly
hadn't been that.

"He doesn't understand what he's saying." The words
tumbled out of her as soon as she recovered her voice.
She was almost incoherent in her desire to offer some
explanation of Andy's disastrous choice of greeting. "The
only man he sees frequently is Joan's husband. The Kra-
kowskis have two-year-old twins, and naturally they call
their father Dadda. Andy must have heard them. He
probably thinks it's the word you're supposed to use
whenever you see a man."

"You don't have to explain. For God's sake, Brooke,
do you consider me such a monster that you think I

wouldn't understand?" Morgan's mouth twisted into a hard smile. "I'd be prepared to wager a large sum of money that 'Dad' is the last thing you wanted him to say to me."

"Walk!" Andy said, providing Brooke with a welcome excuse not to reply. "Go walk. Momma and Dadda." He smiled widely, obviously pleased with the long string of words he had produced so clearly. Sometimes his efforts to fit words together resulted in sentences that were incomprehensible even to his mother. But not today, Brooke thought despairingly. Not today.

"You should call me uncle," Morgan said with sudden decisiveness. "I'm your Uncle Morgan. Can you say uncle?"

Andy looked at Morgan in silence. "Walk," he said at last. "Go walk."

"Okay, okay. We'll go for a walk." Morgan ran his hand through his hair in a gesture of considerable agitation. Brooke fought back a wild urge to giggle. How funny it was that Morgan Kent, unfazed by the biggest and most powerful men in the country, could find himself stumbling and stuttering in the presence of one very small boy.

"Is there a coffee shop near here?" Morgan asked. "I checked out of my hotel without stopping for breakfast this morning, and I could use a cup of coffee. Several cups, in fact."

"I could make you some here," she offered.

"Go walk," Andy repeated for the third time, apparently bored with his long session on his mother's lap. He emphasized his wishes by squirming to the floor and padding across the living room to stand squarely in front of the door. "Go out," he said, smiling at Morgan in gap-toothed anticipation.

"I guess the question has been decided for us," Morgan said. "We're going out for coffee. Don't you find your son's manners a trifle overbearing?"

Brooke looked up quickly, wondering if she had heard a trace of laughter in Morgan's voice. But his face betrayed no sign of amusement, and she warned herself to stop imagining a new vulnerability in his personality. Surely she wasn't crazy enough to hope that Andy would melt Morgan's granite heart. He was far more likely to hate the child than to grow to love him.

"I'll get my coat," she said. Despite all her thoughts of self-warning, she was aware of a tiny, dangerous bubble of pleasure that was forming somewhere deep inside her. She hurried into the bedroom and pulled a jacket out of the closet at random. When she returned to the living room she found Andy clambering into his stroller while Morgan held it steady. She squashed a second irrational flare of hope. Remember, she told herself, this is the child that Morgan ordered you to get rid of. Just because you find Andy's smiles irresistible, Morgan isn't likely to feel the same.

She bumped the stroller down the apartment-house steps, and Andy clapped with approval at each familiar thump. She was starting to push him in the direction of the nearest fast-food outlet when she noticed Morgan's silver-gray Cimarron parked a few yards away.

"Oh, your car! I forgot you must have driven it here," she exclaimed. "You can't leave it parked there."

"Why not? The sign says two-hour parking."

She looked at him and gave a tiny, hard laugh. "This isn't rural Rendford, Morgan. If you leave any car here for two hours—but especially a Cadillac—by the time you come back it'll have been stripped down to the body work, providing it hasn't been ripped off by professional car thieves first, of course."

"Then we'd better drive to a different type of neighborhood where it's safe to park," he said curtly.

She was surprised to hear the note of anger in his

voice. Wasn't he pleased that she'd warned him what could happen to his car? Would he have preferred to return and find it totally vandalized?

"That settles it," Morgan said.

"Settles what?" she asked.

He didn't answer her question. "How the hell can you justify living in a neighborhood that's so dangerous that you can't even park a car?"

"I can justify it very easily. It's the only neighborhood I can afford."

She pretended not to hear the expletive he muttered under his breath. "Get Andy out of his stroller," he ordered. "I'll unlock the car."

She obediently lifted Andy into her arms and collapsed the stroller so that it could be stowed in the car trunk. Then she slipped into the seat next to Morgan, holding Andy on her lap. She realized with a shock of half-rueful amusement that Andy had never before traveled in a private car. Once or twice they had needed to go somewhere by cab, but since his birth she had traveled almost everywhere using some form of public transportation. Nothing, she thought, could more clearly emphasize the gulf between her old, luxurious life with Morgan and the life she had led since Andy's birth.

Andy seemed very pleased with his new surroundings. He patted various knobs and buttons, then stared out of the window at the passing trucks. He was delighted to observe these from a new perspective and kept Brooke busy by pointing to as many of them as he could. "Look truck!" he insisted at regular intervals, and Brooke would oblige by admiring the monster vehicles. After a few minutes, Andy's wriggles started to decrease and he fell asleep, lulled by the unfamiliar rhythm of the car. His head drooped heavily on Brooke's arm. Without saying anything, Morgan lowered the arm rest between them so that she would have a place to rest Andy's weight. She murmured her thanks, surprised that he had noticed her problem.

She had been so preoccupied with Andy that it wasn't until he fell asleep that she took conscious note of where they were going. She knew they were on a highway, and she had automatically assumed Morgan was driving closer to the center of Boston. When she finally paid attention to the signposts, she saw that they were speeding at fifty-five miles per hour in the wrong direction. They were going north.

"Where are you taking me and Andy?" she asked, her voice taut with leashed panic.

"To New Hampshire."

"New Hampshire! Have you gone crazy? Where in New Hampshire?"

There was a short pause. "To my home."

Panic engulfed her. "I won't go! Let me out of this car!"

"Be reasonable, Brooke. You have to see the lawyers some time. It may as well be now."

She refused to listen to the faint note of uncertainty in his voice. She refused to observe the lines of tension that suggested Morgan wasn't quite as self-assured as he was trying to sound. She deliberately goaded herself to anger.

"You tricked me! You *knew* I'd never agree to go back to Kent House, so you kidnapped me. I won't go, Morgan! Turn the car around, or I swear I'll jump out!"

"And what are you planning to do with your son when you jump?" His chill, clipped words cut across her rising hysteria more effectively than a dash of cold water. "Are you going to leave him with me or drop him on the pavement? Which would you consider a worse fate for him, I wonder?"

"Damn you, Morgan! Will you stop this car?"

"No." There was a moment of tense silence during

which Brooke finally acknowledged the rigidity of Morgan's hands on the steering wheel and the heavily scored lines of weariness that ran from his nostrils to his mouth. She knew that he wasn't nearly as calm as he was trying to appear, and the knowledge softened her anger. She turned to stare blindly out the car window. How she resented the way Morgan could still make her respond to him!

"What's all this about, Morgan?" she asked, straining to keep her voice low and calm. "Two years ago you ordered me out of your home. Now you're trying to force me to come back. Why the dramatic change?"

Morgan kept his eyes on the road ahead. "My father hasn't been well since you left Kent House, and the prognosis for his recovery isn't very good. As you can imagine, he's taken Andrew's loss very badly, and I think...your son...would be a great consolation to him. I have good reasons for bringing you to Kent House for a few weeks, Brooke. Would you please come? For my father's sake, if not for mine?"

She shut her ears to the husky note of genuine appeal in his voice. "And what are you planning to tell your father about my son?" she asked with deliberate harshness. "Are you going to introduce him as Andrew's child?"

The grim lines of weariness deepened, and she heard the ragged intake of his breath. "Of course I have no such intention. I'll tell my father that Andy is our son— yours and mine."

She began to laugh then, and once she had started, she couldn't seem able to stop. How incredibly perverse fate could be! Two years ago, when she had been three months pregnant and scared half out of her mind, she would have wept for joy if Morgan had made her such an offer. Now it was all too late.

Her laughter turned to sobs, and she was only half-

aware of Morgan's decisive turn on the steering wheel.
A few minutes later he maneuvered the car into a space
in the parking lot of a giant shopping center.

He handed her a wad of tissues. "Stop crying,
Brooke," he said quietly. "You're frightening Andy."

She saw that Andy was awake, watching her anxiously, and she allowed him to clamber off her lap into
the back seat. She reached in her purse and found the
spare set of old keys he loved to play with. As soon as
he saw that Andy was comfortably occupied, Morgan
spoke to her.

"Would you mind telling me what I said to provoke
that outburst?"

"I was considering the ironies of fate," she said
tightly. "Two years ago, when I told you I was pregnant,
I begged you to believe the baby was yours. I did everything short of crawling on my knees to ask you to accept
that the child was yours. If I'd thought it would change
your mind, I probably *would* have crawled. And what
did you do, Morgan?"

"I made the worst mistake of my life," he replied
softly. "I suggested you have an abortion."

She was so stunned by his reply that she couldn't
speak. She sat staring at her knees until she felt him
place his hand under her chin and gently raise her face
so that he could look into her eyes.

"I made a mistake, Brooke," he said, his gaze never
wavering. "I apologize for it. I should have been more
understanding."

Coldness squeezed out the warmth that had begun to
heal two years of unhappiness. "What do you mean,
Morgan? In what way should you have been more understanding?"

He finally dropped his gaze, his shoulders lifting in
a curious gesture of self-deprecation. "I left you too much
alone and, God knows, I should have learned years ago

that my brother was irresistible to women. You were young . . . naive . . . and I should have been more understanding."

She tore out of his grasp and stumbled out of the car, slamming the door shut behind her. She leaned against the sleek silver hood, clasping her arms around her body in an instinctive gesture of self-protection. She felt physically sick. He still thought Andy was his brother's son. Nothing had changed. Oh God! Why had she sent those flowers?

Anger quickly replaced despair. What was the point of trying to be civil toward Morgan? What was the point of tormenting herself with unspoken hopes? He still believed she had committed adultery with her own brother-in-law. Morgan had never known her, could never have understood her character, if he harbored such a suspicion.

The rage that clouded her mind was quickly replaced with a burning need to hurt Morgan as he had hurt her. She wanted to see him suffer, as she had suffered for two long years. The car door slammed, and she shut her eyes to hide the pain and bitterness she knew he would see in them.

"Brooke, what is it? I didn't mean—"

She cut him off sharply, not sure she could maintain any semblance of poise through another explanation like the last one. "Don't say anything else," she said. "I guess I'm not interested in hearing any apologies. The past is over. It's dead."

As she spoke, he flinched. She saw the hurt that darkened his eyes. She realized that once again he had misunderstood her. For a brief moment her anger cooled. "I've never told you how sorry I am about Andrew," she said quietly. "I know you and your father loved him very much."

"Yes. The plane crash . . . it was a terrible loss to us. Brooke, would—"

"The past doesn't really matter anymore, Morgan," she cut him off again, deliberately hardening her heart by reerecting the barriers of anger. "All I care about now is my son and his future. I'll come to Kent House with you for Andy's sake, and I'll stay for a few weeks if you think that will ease the pain of your father's loss. But I'll leave without a moment's hesitation if anything happens to hurt Andy."

She was aware of the deliberate effort Morgan made to conceal some intense, new emotion. He turned away momentarily. When he looked at her again, his features were rearranged behind a mask of impersonal politeness. She had never known how to penetrate the deliberate blankness of his ice-gray eyes, even though she knew the potential strength of the passions that burned deep in his soul. That was what had made their lovemaking so exquisitely satisfying. The sudden relaxation of all those formidable barriers, the knowledge that she alone could light the fire of a desire that consumed them both.

She forced her mind back from the dangerous abyss of memory.

"My father will be pleased to see you," Morgan said. "And he'll be delighted to hear you've agreed to stay."

"I hope so. And what about Sheila? Is she still living with you?"

Morgan studied her face intently. "My stepsister still lives at Kent House. But she works full time at Kent Industries, so I don't imagine she'll see much of Andy."

Brooke forced herself to sound as calm and rational as he did. "Sheila never liked me, Morgan, although you always refused to believe that. Please make sure she understands that I'll leave Kent House if she threatens Andy's happiness in any way at all."

Morgan was silent for a long time. "You've changed, Brooke," he said at last.

"I've grown up," she snapped. "I'm twenty-six years

old. I'm a woman now, not a young girl."

"I'm very well aware that you're a woman," he said. "I always was."

Heat rippled under her skin, and she recognized the flush of a sexual desire she hadn't felt for two long years. She was glad that working for Tony had taught her how to disguise her true feelings so well. She was confident her face remained expressionless.

Before she replied, a howl of outrage came from the car, and they both sprang to Andy's rescue. He'd reached out too far and had toppled from the back seat onto the floor of the car. Fortunately the thick carpet had cushioned any hurt, except to his dignity, and Brooke soon soothed him with a couple of quick hugs.

Morgan removed the stroller from the trunk, and Brooke strapped Andy into it, taking care not to touch Morgan as she fastened the buckles.

"Walk?" Andy asked hopefully.

"Yes, walk," she agreed.

"Since we're already parked in a shopping center, I thought you could buy anything you need for the next twenty-four hours," Morgan said. "We can pick up the rest of your things on the weekend."

"Yes," she said. "And I'll have to let Tony and Joan know where I am."

"You can call from Kent House." Morgan's voice was as carefully businesslike as her own.

Morgan fell silent, and Brooke pushed Andy toward the entrance of a large department store located at the corner of the parking lot.

The display windows reflected their image—a slender, brown-haired woman; a tall silver-haired man; and a baby whose hair gleamed in the pale sunlight with much the same silver sheen as the man's. Brooke watched their wavering reflection as they headed toward the store. A picture of the perfect family on a shopping trip, she thought. How ironic that the blurred image in the store windows reflected more of the truth than either she or Morgan wanted to acknowledge.

Chapter Four

EARLY THAT AFTERNOON Morgan turned his car into the long driveway of Kent House. The autumn sun gleamed through the branches of the maple trees, lighting the leaves with red fire. Brooke could see a gardener working in a distant corner of the grounds, tending to a bed of golden chrysanthemums. Otherwise, the gardens were deserted. Kent House itself, solid rather than beautiful, stood on the crest of a low rise, appearing dignified and sure of its place after seventy years of changing seasons. It would be hard, Brooke thought, to imagine any greater contrast to the depressing surroundings of her Boston apartment.

On just such a glorious day she had arrived here for the first time, three years ago. Then she had been a shy, immature girl of twenty-three, a graduate student of art history who knew all there was to know about medieval treachery and nothing at all about the more modern forms of betrayal. She had loved Morgan then, with the unshadowed, happy love of a girl who thinks she has found her true love. She had walked into Kent House, laughing and smiling, secure in the warmth of Morgan's devotion.

What a fool she'd been! She hadn't understood that there was more to marriage than moonlight and passion and soft, sweet promises.

Brooke tightened her arms around her son. She was no longer a naive romantic caught in the throes of her first love. She was a somewhat cynical twenty-six-year-old who had grown up overnight when Morgan had ordered her to terminate her pregnancy. If there was anything about the grimness of real life that she hadn't learned while waiting alone for Andy's birth, she had learned it while working at Tony's Bar. Dealing with Tony's brand of customer quickly helped a woman face up to reality. Brooke was confident that she had no trace of any romantic delusions left to weaken her in her dealings with the Kent family. She loved no one but Andy, and after two years of hiding and licking her wounds, she was willing to come out and fight on behalf of her son.

"I expect my father is resting in the living room." Morgan's words broke into her tumbled thoughts. He parked the car in one of the huge garages and stepped out of his seat, coming round quickly to her side of the car.

"Give Andy to me," he said. "I'll carry him into the house."

"I can manage." Instinctively, she clutched Andy closer to her.

"The paving stones in the courtyard might be wet," Morgan said impatiently. "What are you worried about? I'm not planning to abduct him."

Andy, bored with sitting in the gloomy garage, held out his hands for Morgan to pick him up. "Go Dadda," he said. "Go walk."

Brooke noticed the fractional constriction of the muscles in Morgan's jaw when Andy called him Dadda, but his voice was almost expressionless when he said, "I don't think Andy likes the word uncle. Perhaps, in view of what we're planning to tell my father, that's just as well."

"Oh, yes! No doubt it's all for the best in the best of all possible worlds!"

Morgan looked at Brooke intently, and she knew he had picked up the faint thread of hysteria that had come back into her voice. He said nothing, however, simply hoisting Andy into the crook of his arm, leaving one hand free to help her from the car.

She resisted the impulse to push his hand aside and got out of the car as quickly as she could, not allowing herself time to think about the touch of his hand against her skin. "Hadn't you better warn your father that I'm coming?" she asked as they walked across the yard to a side entrance. "I mean, if he's been sick, perhaps the shock will be too much for him."

Morgan was silent as he fumbled in his pocket for the key. He put Andy down but continued to hold firmly onto the child's hand.

"My father knew I was coming to find you," he said finally as the door swung open. "And I . . . telephoned . . . early this morning to let them know you would be coming home with me."

"So you *did* plan it all along!" She stepped into the white-paneled hallway, so angry that she scarcely noticed she was back in a house she had once sworn never to enter again.

"Was there any other way to get you here?"

"The end justifies the means: that's always been your motto, hasn't it, Morgan?"

"Cat!" Andy exclaimed loudly, wrenching his hand from Morgan's grasp. "Big cat! Pretty cat. Nice." He strung all his words of approval together, apparently indifferent to the fact that the cat was neither big nor particularly pretty. He bent down and tried to capture the fat gray kitten between his tiny fists. The cat, its tail roughly jerked by Andy's inexpert fingers, arched its back and spat warningly. Andy's eyes grew round with astonishment, and the cat seized its opportunity to wriggle away and streak off in the direction of the kitchen. Andy sat down with a bump of surprise, and both Morgan and Brooke burst out with sympathetic laughter.

Andy scrambled to his feet and would have set off in immediate pursuit if Brooke hadn't restrained him. "Cat come here!" Andy protested.

"Later," Brooke promised.

Andy thrust out his lower lip in a rebellious pout, glancing at Morgan out of the corner of his eyes.

"Your mother said later," Morgan remarked quietly.

Andy's gaze locked with Morgan's, then, without another word, he took Brooke's hand and hopped along between the two adults in the direction of the living room.

"We weren't allowed animals of any sort in the apartment," Brooke explained. "That's why he finds them so fascinating."

"Perhaps we should get him a puppy while he's here. Or is he too young for that?"

"I'm sure he's too young. But thank you for the thought."

"What a delightful family group!" The silvery feminine voice seemed warm with welcome. "Brooke, how marvelous to see you again! You're looking so well ...considering...er...everything. And this must be your son."

"Hello, Sheila." The laughter she had shared with Morgan vanished from Brooke's eyes, and her hand tightened protectively around Andy's fingers. She knew Morgan was watching her closely, knew that he disapproved of her cold response to his stepsister's welcome.

With considerable effort Brooke stretched her lips into a smile. She wouldn't let Sheila win again this time. She wasn't going to let her stepsister-in-law isolate her in the household so that even the servants thought she was either neurotic or hopelessly inadequate.

"It's good to be back," she said, using every ounce of her self-control to make her voice sound light and pleasant. "I'm sorry that it required such a tragic occasion to...to bring me here. I know how deeply you feel Andrew's loss."

Sheila's blue eyes darkened with genuine pain. Brooke remembered that she had always been close to Andrew, treating him with a light-hearted, sisterly affection. That affection was one of the reasons Morgan refused to believe that Sheila's feelings for him were anything other than those of a sister for an older brother.

"Why do you always insist that Sheila is in love with me?" Morgan had asked Brooke after one of their bitter arguments. "Why can't you see that her feelings for me are no different from her feelings for my brother?"

"Andrew is six years younger than you," Brooke had replied, knowing Morgan wasn't really listening to her. "Sheila was thirteen and Andrew was fourteen when her mother married your father. You were nearly twenty. Can't you understand that Sheila saw Andrew as another child, the friend and brother she'd never had? But *you* were a man! When you came home from college, you must have seemed the incarnation of every adolescent fantasy she had ever had." But Morgan had rejected her opinions. Perceptive as he was in most situations, where his family was concerned he seemed to Brooke to be utterly blind.

"I can't believe Andrew is gone forever." Sheila's shaky voice interrupted Brooke's all-too-vivid memories, and Brooke could hear the grief that thickened her stepsister-in-law's voice.

"It's a terrible loss for the whole family," Brooke said

quietly. She felt more sympathetic toward Sheila than she ever had in the past. Sheila's mother had died only a couple of years after marrying Mr. Kent. Her stepsister-in-law, Brooke reflected, had suffered considerable unhappiness in her short life. She reached out and touched Sheila's arm in a brief, instinctive gesture of comfort.

For a moment Sheila's hard features softened, then, with a quick shake of her hair, she dashed away a trace of tears. "Father is waiting in the living room, Morgan," she said. "I know he'll be pleased to see you. He's been on pins and needles ever since I told him you'd called."

"You explained that I was bringing home . . . my son?"

My son. A flash of intense emotion shivered down Brooke's spine, but she wasn't sure whether she felt pleasure or pain at hearing Morgan publicly claim Andy as his.

"Father knows about the child," Sheila said. "The fact that he has a grandson to meet is just about all that's kept him going today."

"We'll go in." Morgan moved decisively toward the living room doors, but Brooke hesitated, unsure if she was ready to meet Mr. Kent again after two years of painful separation. She was surprised to feel Morgan's arm around her waist, urging her forward with a gentle but impersonal touch. Sensitive to atmosphere, Andy seemed to guess at Brooke's tension and clung to her jeans fearfully, which was unlike his normally outgoing nature.

"Come along, Andy," Morgan said calmly. With only a tiny show of reluctance, Andy released his clutch on Brooke's legs and took Morgan's hand.

The first thing Brooke saw as they entered the living room was a blazing fire in the huge marble fireplace. It was probably intended to create an illusion of cheer, she surmised, but any hint of cheerfulness was singularly lacking from the thin, drooping figure seated in front of the glowing logs. Brooke remembered the aggressive, hot-tempered man her father-in-law had been, and she was appalled to see how two brief years had changed him.

He glanced up as they approached his chair, and Brooke was relieved to find that sickness and grief hadn't removed all the sparkle from his eyes. He glowered at her from beneath eyebrows that were as thick, white, and bushy as they had been before.

"You've taken your own sweet time to let me know I'm a grandfather," he said as soon as Brooke was within range of his formidable scowl.

She was amazed at how glad she was to see him again, and she had little difficulty in squashing the angry retort that sprang to her lips. She hurried to his side and knelt down beside his chair. "I'm sorry," she said. "I had no right to deprive you of your own grandson . . . your first grandchild. But it was so difficult for me to know what I ought to do."

He took the hand she held out to him in a brief clasp, and Brooke saw with dismay that his fingers shook with weakness as he grasped her hand.

"Well, you're here now," he said. "Where's that grandson of mine? I may as well take a good look at him now that you've finally condescended to bring him back where he belongs."

Morgan stepped forward immediately. "This is Andy," he said. If she hadn't known better, Brooke would have sworn she detected a note of pride in Morgan's voice. "Say how do you do to your grandfather," he instructed.

Andy stepped forward without much reluctance, and Brooke blessed the fact that circumstances had trained him to welcome meetings with new people. "Hi Dadda," he said cheerfully, displaying all eight of his teeth in a broad grin. "Dadda look cat."

"Do you think he's trying to tell me I look like a cat?"

Mr. Kent asked. His voice was brusque, but his eyes shone suspiciously as he picked Andy up with Morgan's help and deposited the child on his knee.

Andy immediately wriggled back down to the floor. "Get cat," he said, heading for the living room door at a spanking trot. Brooke managed to grab him as he went past.

"You can see the cat later," she said. "Andy, this is your grandfather. Can you say Grandpa?"

Andy didn't bother to answer. Brooke could imagine his thoughts. Nobody had ever mentioned grandfathers to him before, and he had little interest in learning about them when he was in a house that possessed such treasures as a gray cat and a long hallway clearly designed for running and sliding.

"I'll find the cat for you," Mr. Kent said. "Come here and look at my watch while we're waiting for the cat to be brought in."

Andy eyed his grandfather speculatively. "Cat come here?" he asked, apparently making quite sure that he had understood.

"Yes." Mr. Kent nodded. "Would you be kind enough to find us a cat, please, Sheila?"

"Bribery, Father?" she asked.

"Certainly." Mr. Kent gave a rueful shrug. "I'm getting old, and I'm beginning to show signs of wisdom at last. I'm not too proud to resort to bribes if I can't get what I want by any other method. I can assure you that pride makes a mighty cold companion on a winter's night."

Sheila started to make some comment, then apparently changed her mind. "I'll see if I can find the kitten," she said, leaving the room without another word.

Mr. Kent watched his stepdaughter's departure, then turned back to scrutinize Brooke. "You look tired and pale," he said with unwelcome frankness. "Make sure

Morgan gives you a chance to relax a little now that you've come home." He didn't wait for her to reply, but gently pulled Andy closer to his chair, taking out a silver pocket watch and flipping open the back. "Listen," he said, holding the watch to his grandson's ear.

A slow smile spread across Andy's face, and he reached out to grab the watch. Mr. Kent held it just out of reach, allowing Andy to see the tiny clockwork wheels that spun with solid regularity inside the silver case.

Andy's face showed his fascination, and Mr. Kent touched him very lightly on the cheek. "He's the image of you, Morgan," he said softly, then gave a bark of friendly laughter. "He didn't inherit much in the way of looks from you, Brooke, did he? He looks about ninety-eight percent pure Morgan Kent."

Brooke's cheeks paled even further, and she could feel the tension radiating from Morgan's corner of the room. She held her breath, waiting in an agony of suspense to hear what he might say.

He didn't even look at her. "Andy is certainly like our side of the family," he said evenly. "But don't you think he looks more like Andrew than like me?"

If Mr. Kent was aware of the heightened tension in the room, he gave no sign of it. After carefully closing his watch, he returned it to his inner vest pocket. "Not at all," he said when the watch was safely away. "Naturally, you don't remember how you looked as a baby, or even as a young boy. But, in fact, Andy is the image of you at the same age. I must search for my baby-picture albums and show you both some photographs."

Sheila reentered the room at that moment, carrying the gray kitten in her arms. "Here you are, Andy," she said. "This is Joshua. Take care you don't hurt him."

"Josh," Andy said with a huge grin. He surprised everybody by managing to scoop up the cat and stagger across the room, where he dumped the protesting animal on his grandfather's lap. "Look cat!" he commanded.

Mr. Kent bit off an exclamation of pain as the cat's claws came into contact with his legs. "He sure is a handsome fellow. See, Andy, you stroke him this way. Give me your hand and I'll show you how to make the cat lie down."

Andy willingly placed his fingers within his grand-father's frail clasp. Together they stroked the kitten until it gave a contented, growling purr.

"The crib you asked me to order from the local store has been delivered, Morgan," Sheila said, unconcealed irritation in her voice. What at? Brooke wondered. Did she resent Andy's immediate rapport with his grandfather?

"Thank you." Morgan's features were tightly shut-tered, and he seemed to find some difficulty in tearing his gaze away from Andy. "Has the crib been set up yet?" he asked Sheila.

"Yes. It's in Brooke's bedroom, as you suggested."

"Would you like to come upstairs to your room? I expect you'd like the chance to rest before dinner." Mor-gan's voice was so impersonal that he might as well have been talking to an acquaintance he'd met only recently.

"Yes, I would like to rest." Brooke's politeness matched Morgan's. "But what about Andy?"

"I'm capable of looking after my own grandson," Mr. Kent interjected. "And if we grow tired of one another, there's a fully qualified nurse lurking in my bedroom, just waiting to take charge of us both. You go and rest, my girl. Take the chance while you can. Morgan tells me you've been working nights?"

"Yes," Brooke said. "I had to. There was no room at the local day-care center, so it was all I could do."

Morgan's mouth tightened ominously, but Sheila spoke before he could say whatever was on his mind. "There are a lot of messages for you, Morgan, which I think you should answer. I've tried to stall people as best I could, but I think you ought to call in at the office. Your secretary is going crazy. I can take Brooke to her room, if you like. There's no need for you to do it."

"Kent Industries won't collapse if I take one more afternoon off," Morgan said. "I'll deal with the urgent messages this evening. Are you coming, Brooke?"

She followed him out of the room and up the stairs, keeping her eyes fixed rigidly ahead when she came to the suite of rooms Morgan had shared with her during their marriage. Neither of them made any comment as they passed the door of the suite and Morgan ushered her into one of the guest rooms.

Brooke recognized it from her previous stay at Kent House. The room was large and pleasant, tastefully decorated in neutral shades. Brooke remembered that a private bathroom opened off to the right. A solid maplewood crib was already standing in a corner of the room, and a pile of fluffy white blankets rested neatly at one end of the crib. How easy life was when you had money, Brooke thought. How easy it was when all you had to do was pick up the phone and whatever you needed arrived at the door as fast as the delivery truck could get from the store to your house.

"Is everything to your satisfaction?" Morgan asked. His voice held a tinge of irony, and Brooke wondered just how much of her thoughts he was still able to read. He had always teased her about her lack of interest in the Kent family financial affairs, saying she hadn't outgrown the attitudes of her student days. In a way he'd been right. It wasn't until she had a newborn infant to feed and clothe that she'd realized for the first time what financial stability could actually mean. She forced her wandering thoughts back to the present.

"Everything's fine," she acknowledged.

"I thought you would prefer that Andy stay with you

at first. Later, he can have a room of his own."

"Later! Morgan, what do you mean? How long do you expect this charade to continue? I have a life of my own to lead . . . a career—"

"A career! Do you call what you did at Tony's Bar a *career?* What happened to all your ambitions about working in an art museum?"

"They met with reality," she said curtly. "I needed money and I found out that nightclubs pay better than museums. And art museums don't want you to work at night."

"Why didn't you ask somebody for help? What about . . . Andrew . . . if you weren't prepared to come to me."

She directed a cool, level gaze at him. "I refuse to start this discussion again," she said tightly. "Andrew is dead, and you and I are divorced, so it's all irrelevant now."

He walked over to the window and gazed out over the expanse of empty gardens. "We're not divorced," he said quietly.

For a moment she couldn't seem to attach meaning to his words. She stared at him in blank silence, then slowly recovered her power of speech.

"Of course we're divorced," she corrected him, refusing to acknowledge the strange way her stomach had lurched.

"Did you divorce me? If so, how? I haven't signed any papers. And *I* couldn't divorce *you* because I didn't know where you were."

She knew that what he was saying made sense, but she refused to accept his words. For two years she had tried to tell herself that her marriage to Morgan was over. Dead. Now it seemed she might have to face the fact that legally they were still husband and wife. Her voice shook when she spoke again. "I assumed that with all that Kent money you would manage to find some lawyer to buy you out of such an inconvenient marriage." She swallowed hard, fighting back panic. "Naturally I assumed you had divorced me, that you'd gone to Mexico or Reno, or somewhere. You *must* have."

"No."

The flatness of his denial fell into the sudden silence, and she felt her throat close up at his uncompromising statement. She looked frantically around the room, then rushed to the doorway, as if by putting a greater distance between Morgan and herself she could deny the truth.

He moved so swiftly that she didn't realize what he was doing until she saw him interposed between herself and the door.

"I want to leave," she said through tight lips. "I want to take Andy and go back to my apartment." Her voice rose on a note of desperation. "I won't be married to you anymore! I couldn't stand it. Not again!"

"Why not?" His hands gripped her loosely, not really barring her exit because he didn't need to restrain her physically. Now that their bodies were so close, she was trapped by the memory of her own emotions. She remembered so many occasions like this one, times when they had provoked each other's anger without knowing how or why.

She remembered the inevitable aftermath, too. She had always possessed one weapon that left Morgan helpless. He had never been able to control the intense physical awareness they had for each other. Even when he felt most alienated from her, she had only to move into his arms and the flame of sexuality would flare between them. She remembered how his cold gray eyes would darken with a storm cloud of angry passion, and she remembered the fierce pleasure she derived from watching his anger dissolve into naked desire, which melted into a fire that consumed them both.

Her body softened at the memory, and hot color flooded into her cheeks.

Morgan moved away from her with a convulsive jerk,

dropping his hands to his side and balling them into tight fists, but he didn't leave the room.

"Perhaps it would be better if we discussed this some other time," he said.

"What's the matter, Morgan?" she taunted him softly, strangely triumphant at the knowledge that he still found her desirable. Her feelings were in tumult. She wanted to hurt him and make him crave her body all at the same time. "Don't you want to hear the truth? Don't you like to be reminded that I found marriage to you—the great Morgan Kent of Kent Industries, Incorporated—hell on earth?"

"I don't think we should discuss this right now. You're tired . . . we're both tired. It would be better if we didn't say things we'll regret later."

"I can hardly believe what I'm hearing," Brooke mocked, only part of her attention on what she was saying. She felt Morgan's eyes riveted on her body and guessed that he could see the swell of her breasts clearly beneath the thin wool of her sweater.

She tossed her hair out of her eyes and watched the faint flicker of emotion that crossed Morgan's carefully controlled features. "Are you actually suggesting that you can be provoked into doing something you might regret later?" she asked softly.

"I despise you, Brooke," he said thickly, dragging his eyes away from her at last. "And I despise the uses to which you put that highly desirable body of yours. Is that what you wanted to hear me say? Are you satisfied now?"

His words should have humiliated her, but instead she was filled with an exhilarating sense of power. "You're a liar, Morgan," she said. "You don't despise me. You desire me."

He flushed darkly under the tightly drawn skin of his cheekbones. "You were a sickness with me, Brooke.

When I met you, it was as if I had a fever and couldn't see the real person that you were. But I'm cured now."

"Are you?" she murmured. "Are you sure?"

She had moved so close to him that his harsh breathing fanned her cheeks. She could tell just how much effort it was costing him to hold his body away from hers. She looked up at him through her long lashes, and for a moment she forgot all her calculation as their eyes met. As her lips parted in unspoken invitation, she forgot all the good reasons she had for keeping him at a safe distance. She forgot how their lovemaking had always been a two-edged sword that tormented her as effectively as it tormented Morgan. She remembered only that she was a woman who had once loved this man with every particle of her being.

"Morgan . . ." she said huskily, tracing the outline of his mouth with one tentative finger.

His iron self-control suddenly snapped. His hands circled her waist, and he pulled her against his body in a sharp, savage embrace. His mouth was hot and aggressive when it covered hers, and she responded with a passion that matched his own, even though she knew there was nothing of love or compassion in his angry kisses. Her mouth opened to the thrust of his tongue, and she swayed in his arms, weak with the longing to surrender to his lovemaking. The heat and passion of his kisses overwhelmed her. The pain as he crushed her body against him was in itself an exquisite form of pleasure.

When one of his hands slipped under her sweater and closed around the fullness of her breast, she remembered, almost too late, that if they made love she would be allowing Morgan to tear apart her soul—while he would merely be fulfilling a moment of physical desire. She twisted her head away from the sweet savagery of his mouth and pushed his hand away from her breast.

"Stop, Morgan," she said shakily. "Stop right now."

"Isn't it what you wanted?" he asked, and his voice was grim. "I thought you were begging for a little love-making to fill in a boring afternoon. I'm sorry if I misread the signals."

"I want a divorce," she said, moving away from him and shutting her ears to his cruel remarks. She tried to control the harsh, uneven rhythm of her breathing. "It was a mistake to agree to this visit, and I'll leave to-morrow. I'll see the lawyers first about your brother's will, and I'll ask them to draw up a divorce agreement for you to sign. I realize that Andy should be allowed to visit his grandfather regularly, and I'll write that into the divorce agreement if you'd prefer to have my consent in writing."

Morgan looked at her coolly. "I'll fight you for custody of Andy."

"What?"

"You heard what I said. I'll claim custody of Andy as my son if you set divorce proceedings into motion."

"But you don't believe he's your son! You've never accepted Andy as your child! How can you claim custody?"

"Apart from you, nobody has any idea that I ever rejected Andy. As far as the courts and my family are concerned, I didn't know he existed until two days ago. How do you think a judge would view that piece of information?"

"You wouldn't do it. You couldn't take Andy away from me. You wouldn't want to."

"I could and I will. I think a lawyer could make pretty good use of the fact that you hid my own son from me for two years. I'd say my chances of getting custody are pretty good."

"Your son! You're threatening to claim Andy is your son!" She started to laugh, then clamped her lips together, biting them until she could taste the blood in her mouth.

"Why?" She barely managed to squeeze out the question.

He turned from her with a slight shrug. "My father is old, sick, and grieving. I think he deserves some uninterrupted time with his only grandchild—"

She interrupted him. "I didn't mean that. I meant, why are you doing this to me? To both of us. . . . You know I won't start divorce proceedings if there's a chance I might lose Andy. Don't you want to be free?"

"Free. . . . That's certainly a wonderful thought." Morgan's voice and expression were equally flat and completely at variance with his words. "If you don't want to risk losing Andy, I suggest you accustom yourself to the idea of a long stay at Kent House."

"I can't bear the thought of spending time in the same house with you! I can't bear it, do you hear?"

"If you remember, my dear Brooke, one of your prime complaints during the brief months of our marriage was that I was never home. According to you, I worked far too many hours a day, and at a profession that wasn't worthy of anybody's time or attention. Computers, you told me, are the destroyers of mankind's soul. Nothing has changed, Brooke. I still work twelve hours a day, six days a week. And at the moment, as it happens, Kent Industries is threatened with a takeover bid by a consortium of unknown buyers. Even I admit that I've been putting in somewhat excessive office hours recently. Don't worry, my dear. You'll hardly see me, even if you do stay on at Kent House."

She couldn't make complete sense of his explanation. "Would you get out of my room?" she said. "I need to sleep before dinner."

He scrutinized her pale face for a moment, then turned abruptly and left without saying anything else. She waited until the door slammed shut behind him, then kicked off her shoes and fell on the bed in a haze of fatigue and worry. Sheer black fright swept through her at the possibility of losing Andy. Surely Morgan's threats to claim custody hadn't been serious. What had she let herself in for? Would she have sent those flowers if she could have foreseen what would happen?

She found no immediate answer to her silent questions and stirred restlessly on the soft bed. Her lips felt tender from the brutal force of Morgan's kisses. She touched her fingers to her mouth with a shiver of vivid recollection. She could still feel his arms wrapped around her body, pulling her roughly against his chest, and she shook with the intensity of her remembered feelings.

She tried to shut out the unwelcome images and rolled over onto her stomach, burying her face in the feathery darkness of the pillows. But it was impossible to sleep when her conscious mind required her to fight constantly against admitting the truth. At last she abandoned the struggle and allowed the subconscious knowledge to come to the surface of her mind. The truth was that during those bleak hours when she had believed Morgan was dead, she had been brought face to face with the stark reality of her own feelings. When she had thought Morgan was dead, she had admitted that she still loved him.

Brooke lifted her head from the protection of the pillows and stared blindly at the room. She forced herself to face the truth. She had spent the last two years hiding, not from her husband but from herself. She loved Morgan Kent, and none of their misunderstandings, none of his subtle cruelty, seemed capable of destroying that love.

Chapter Five

ANDY, SCRUBBED AND SMELLING of talcum powder, rattled the sides of his crib, chuckling to himself as he bounced up and down on the springy new mattress.

"Nice cat," he said to Brooke. "Big. Nice."

"The nice cat has gone to bed," Brooke said. "Now you have to go to bed, too, otherwise you'll be too tired to play with the cat tomorrow morning."

Andy stuck his thumb in his mouth and looked at her in silence. "Dadda's cat," he remarked somewhat inaudibly. He removed his thumb from his mouth just long enough to add, "Dadda big. Nice. Pretty."

Despite her nervous tension, Brooke laughed as she hugged her son. "Well, I'm not sure *pretty* is the right word to use, Andy. But your daddy certainly is big." And powerful, she thought. And damnably, terrifyingly attractive.

She walked over to Andy's crib, tucking the blankets tightly around him. "Sleep time," she said firmly.

"Mommy is going to eat dinner now, but I'll be close by."

She was glad Andy didn't seem disturbed by his new surroundings. His grandfather had unearthed a shabby teddy bear from the corner of some closet, and Andy had accepted this gift with enthusiasm. As he snuggled beneath the covers, he clutched the faded blue blanket he took everywhere, and Brooke was touched to see him unfold one very small corner and drape it awkwardly over the teddy bear's protruding tummy.

"Teddy go sleep. Cat go sleep," he murmured.

"Yes, and now you must go to sleep, too." Brooke turned out all the lights until the room was illuminated by only the dim glow of a single night light. Andy jostled around beneath his covers for a few minutes and then dropped off to sleep, in the middle of a wriggle. Brooke pulled the covers over his shoulders. He lay on his tummy, with one arm flung protectively over the teddy bear, his bottom sticking up in the air.

Brooke's reverie was disturbed by a soft knock on the bedroom door. She opened it and discovered a short, pleasant-looking young woman standing on the other side.

"Mrs. Kent?" The woman scarcely waited for Brooke's nod before continuing in a low voice. "I'm Angela Finks, Mr. Kent's nurse. I met Andy this afternoon while you were resting. My room is just across the corridor from this one, and I'll be happy to keep an eye on your son while you eat dinner. If you would like me to, that is."

"Why, thank you, I'd really appreciate that. Andy doesn't usually wake up, but since these are strange surroundings..."

"You'd like to feel doubly sure," the nurse completed Brooke's unfinished sentence. "Mrs. Kent, could you come into my room for a moment so that we can talk without waking Andy?"

"Of course." Brooke followed the nurse across the hallway into another of the guest rooms. This one was decorated in shades of peach, and every available surface was covered with photographs of laughing children.

Angela Finks noticed Brooke's interest and smiled. "I'm the youngest in a family of five children," she said. "I already have ten nephews and nieces, with two more on the way, so you see I'm well qualified to look after Andy for you, Mrs. Kent."

"More qualified than me! And please call me Brooke."

"Thank you. I wanted to let you know what a wonderful tonic your son has been for Mr. Kent. I don't know if you're aware that Mr. Kent is suffering from a rare form of adult-onset diabetes. With medication and constant supervision of his diet there's no real reason why his condition shouldn't stabilize. However, to be perfectly honest with you, Brooke, I've been here for two months and Mr. Kent has seemed indifferent to the state of his health. When we heard the terrible news about Andrew's death, I was afraid he would give up the struggle to regain his health. I can't describe the change in Mr. Kent since you brought Andy here. This afternoon he ate and drank exactly what he was supposed to, and he was actually fussing about how soon he'd be strong enough to take Andy on a day trip. He said something about going fishing. It's the first time he's *wanted* to go outside the house since I arrived here."

"I'm very glad we cheered him up," Brooke said quietly. "This is a sad time for him and his family, and I'm pleased he enjoys Andy's company so much." Her expression must have revealed that her words weren't entirely true, because Angela looked at her shrewdly.

"I realize I'm stepping way out of my professional position, but it would be great if you felt able to stay for a few months. Mr. Kent needs to have his grandson near him."

Brooke jerked to her feet. "I don't know how long we'll be staying, Angela. But I promise that whatever happens, I'll bring Andy back for frequent visits."

"That would certainly help."

Brooke smiled wanly. "It's the best I can promise, I'm afraid." She glanced hurriedly at her watch, anxious to change the subject. "Heavens, I'm late for dinner. Don't you usually join the family for your meals?"

"Sometimes, but tonight I've decided to babysit. Playing with Andy this afternoon reminded me of how much I like young children. I miss all my noisy nephews and nieces when I've been away from them too long. When I'm with them, of course, all I can think about is how wonderful it would be to have a job somewhere quiet—like a desert island, maybe!"

Brooke laughed, glad that she was able to leave Andy in the care of someone so warm and capable. She took one last peek at her sleeping child before walking slowly down the stairs. She had attended too many dinners at Kent House to be under any illusions about what was in store for her. When she had first married Morgan she had been overwhelmed by the formality of the Kent family dinners. Comfortable meals around her grandmother's kitchen table hadn't prepared her to deal with acres of white linen and rows of shiny table silver. She had begged Morgan to let her prepare simple meals that the two of them could share in their own rooms, but he had always refused. Brooke often felt that she hadn't just married Morgan but the entire Kent family and their domestic servants, too.

She glanced nervously in a hall mirror as she walked past. She was wearing a pleated plaid skirt and pale blue sweater she had bought at the shopping center that morning. The colors were flattering but sedate. Brooke tried to tell herself that she wasn't trying to look sexy, but she knew that was a lie. She wanted Morgan to think she was still beautiful. More than that, she wanted him to find her desirable. She pushed all such useless thoughts out of her mind as she walked into the family dining room.

She saw Morgan as soon as she opened the door, and her feet hesitated for a fraction of a second as she registered the full impact of his presence. Dressed in dark but casual clothes, he looked taller and more attractive than ever. A concealed overhead light caught the silver highlights of his hair, and the contrast with his deep tan caused Brooke to shiver with familiar physical awareness.

His gaze locked with hers for a brief, silent moment before he turned back to the bar and continued to pour a drink. "Is Andy settled for the night?" he asked, handing Sheila the drink he had just made.

"Yes, thank you. He seems very content," Brooke replied.

"What an obliging baby, to be sure! It seems to me that you can dump . . . er . . . put him anywhere and he'll accept it." Sheila's voice grated on Brooke's raw nerves. "I suppose the poor little boy is used to being left alone? I don't suppose you were able to spend much time with him."

"Andy has never been left alone in his life," Brooke replied tersely. "He's not shy of new surroundings, though, because he's had to learn to meet a wide variety of people."

"And that's a skill you can't learn too early," Morgan's father acknowledged. "Do you want a drink, Brooke? If so, Morgan should fix it for you right away. I know the housekeeper is waiting to serve dinner."

"I'll just have wine with the meal," Brooke said as Mr. Kent pressed the bell to summon the housekeeper.

The servant had scarcely set bowls of lobster bisque in front of each of them before Sheila began a long, involved story about her most recent meeting with the head of the research department at Kent Industries. Her conversation was highly technical, and Brooke understood less than one word in twenty. Mr. Kent looked as if he didn't understand much more.

Morgan made no effort to switch the trend of Sheila's conversation, although once or twice he asked his father to confirm some piece of financial information. Brooke might as well have been a lump of wood for all her presence contributed to the table talk.

After fifteen minutes of silent eating, Brooke began to lose her temper. It was one thing to accept that Morgan and Sheila needed to catch up on a few essential pieces of business. It was another thing to endure an entire meal of technological gossip. She flashed an angry glare at Morgan and was surprised to see a warning flash into his eyes. He gave a slight, almost imperceptible shake of his head and turned his gaze briefly toward his father.

Brooke followed the direction of his eyes. Mr. Kent, she realized with dismay, was hanging on to his self-control by the merest thread. He had eaten almost nothing, and at every pause in the rapid technical talk his features tightened with grief.

Brooke hurriedly looked back at her own plate, flushing with embarrassment at her lack of understanding. Sheila, she realized belatedly, was keeping up this babble of conversation in order to direct Mr. Kent's thoughts away from his son's death. Brooke squirmed uncomfortably on her chair as she realized how ready she had been to misunderstand Sheila. She was becoming so self-centered, so obsessed with the problems of her relationship with Morgan, that she had forgotten that this was probably the first family dinner Mr. Kent had attended since hearing of the plane crash.

Brooke glanced covertly at her stepsister-in-law, aware that her feelings were settling into their old state of uneasy ambivalence. Maybe she was wrong about Sheila, she thought for the hundredth time. Maybe she just imagined that Sheila disliked her. Brooke turned her attention back to her meal and chewed determinedly on a slice of tender roast beef that simply wouldn't slide down her throat. Oh, Andy, she thought, even for your sake I don't know how much more of this I can stand.

Brooke wasn't surprised when Mr. Kent excused himself as soon as the dishes from the main course had been cleared away.

"I'm not supposed to drink coffee or eat dessert," he said with an attempt at a smile. "My dragon of a nurse will scold me if I eat any of that chocolate cake, so if you'll excuse me, I'll take myself upstairs, where I'll be out of temptation's reach."

"I've met your dragon nurse," Brooke said with a smile. "I can't believe her anger's very fierce. She looked pretty tenderhearted to me when she volunteered to keep an eye on Andy."

Mr. Kent smiled back, and his eyes brightened. "Perhaps I'll look at my grandson before I go to bed," he said. "I won't wake him if I go into his room, will I, Brooke?"

"Not at all," she said, relieved to see some animation creep back into her father-in-law's face. "Perhaps you'll give Andy a kiss for me?"

"My pleasure. Good night, all of you."

They all remained silent once Mr. Kent had left the room. Morgan broke the stillness by looking at Brooke and remarking impersonally, "I imagine you'll want to see the lawyers first thing tomorrow morning. Mr. Barnes is dealing with Andrew's affairs. I'll arrange to have a car for you. You'll have to drive because their offices are in Boston."

"Thank you."

"It was certainly a shock to all of us when we learned

that Andrew had left almost everything he possessed to you, Brooke." Sheila gave another of her breathless little laughs, which were apparently intended to remove the sting from her words. "Although I guess we shouldn't have been so surprised. You always did have a very special relationship with my brother, didn't you?"

Brooke bit back her anger, determined not to show it. "I hope Andrew thought of me as someone special. We spent a lot of time together, and I think he confided in me because I was the only other person in this house who wasn't in love with a computer system. He worked with computers because the family expected him to, but he never had the same sense of purpose that the rest of you have. Andrew would always choose to spend the evening with a woman—preferably a beautiful young woman—rather than catch up on his office memos. He liked to dance and sail and ski and eat at fashionable restaurants. Perhaps those weren't very worthwhile pursuits in your eyes, but he was kind. He wanted the people around him to be as happy as he was. When he discovered how many nights I spent alone, he asked me to go out with him." She looked up to see Morgan's accusing gaze riveted on her, and with a surge of defiance, she added, "I liked Andrew and I enjoyed his company. I thought of him as the brother I'd never had." She didn't know if she was glad or sorry when she saw Morgan's frown deepen into a dark scowl.

"Even so, you never told him you had a child," Sheila commented.

"No, I never told him. I wish...I wish now that I had."

As the impact of Brooke's words sank in, a tense silence enveloped the room. Andrew was gone, finally and irretrievably.

Sheila gulped visibly and hurriedly changed the subject. "I can't imagine what it must have been like for you trying to support your child all alone. Morgan tells me you were working in a singles bar and that the place had a *strip* show!"

"Yes, it did, and from what several of the customers told me, I guess it was a good one. Tony, my boss, hired only the most talented dancers, and he made sure they had beautiful bodies."

Sheila stared at Brooke. "I can't believe you're the same girl who told us your professional training would be ruined forever if Morgan wouldn't let you take a part-time job at the art museum! And then you left here to work in a strip club, of all places!"

"Nightclubs pay better than art museums," Brooke said. "And I discovered that babies need to eat regularly in order to stay healthy. It's amazing how easy it was to change my opinions."

Sheila's voice softened and a brief gleam of sympathy flashed in her eyes. "You needed help, Brooke. Why didn't you get in touch with any of us?"

"I felt Andy was my responsibility since I'd chosen to leave Kent House," Brooke said. She was aware of Morgan's gaze scrutinizing her, and she met the icy inspection of his gray eyes with another touch of defiance. "Morgan made it plain to me before I left... that is, when I left Morgan, I realized I had to learn to take care of myself. By working only at night I was able to spend a fair part of every day with my baby. Maybe he missed out on a few expensive toys, but he seems to have developed into a secure and happy toddler."

"You've forgotten one important deprivation," Morgan interjected harshly. "He never saw his father."

"I didn't know his father wanted to see him," Brooke replied hotly. "Anyway, he's seeing you now."

Morgan swallowed the remainder of a large whiskey in a single gulp. "So he is," he said, and Brooke was only too aware of the underlying irony of his words.

After several uneasy moments Sheila broke the tense silence. "If nobody wants any more coffee, I suggest we give the kitchen staff a chance to clear up." She pushed back her chair, glanced hesitantly at Morgan, and walked quickly to the door. "If you two don't mind, I have some personal accounts to settle up. Will you excuse me?" She didn't wait for a reply, but left the room, trailing a waft of expensive perfume.

Brooke would have followed her, but Morgan prevented her. "Come into the living room," he said. "I want to talk to you."

Brooke followed him and stood stiffly in front of the living room fire, unable to think of a single word to say.

"Would you like a drink?" he asked curtly.

"No, thank you."

The silence returned as he poured himself another neat whiskey. Brooke watched, mesmerized, as Morgan swallowed several hefty gulps. What would his lips taste like, she wondered, if he kissed her now? She tried to push the errant question out of her mind, but her eyes became fixed on the firm outline of his mouth, and she felt her throat turn suddenly dry.

Morgan put his glass down on a side table with a faint thud. "What exactly did you do at Tony's?" he asked, and she was startled by the suppressed violence in his voice.

"I was a hostess. The senior hostess, in fact."

"Did you ever work in his strip show?"

"Does it matter to you if I did?"

He turned away, picking up the glass and tossing back the remainder of his whiskey. "Why should it matter to me? You're an adult, so I guess you can display your body to whomever you please."

Brooke had no idea why she suddenly felt the need to tell him the truth. "I worked as a hostess at Tony's, Morgan. Nothing more, ever."

Her expression softened as she made the admission, and for a moment she detected an answering tenderness in his gaze. She took a few hesitant steps toward him and his hard mouth curved into a faint smile before the familiar mask descended once again, wiping his features into cool blankness. "That seems a waste of a stunning body," he said indifferently. "I'm surprised Tony allowed you to conceal such a valuable asset. He didn't strike me as much of a philanthropist."

The distant ringing of a telephone forestalled her furious retort. "Excuse me," Morgan said abruptly. "That call is on my personal line."

He walked out of the room, leaving Brooke torn between rage and tears. He had always produced this effect on her, and two years of added maturity didn't seem to be helping as much as she thought it should.

She walked slowly up the stairs to her room. Morgan hadn't even said why he wanted to speak to her, she realized. It couldn't have been about her work at Tony's, because there was no reason why he should be interested. Damn him and the power he had to disrupt her peaceful life!

She entered her bedroom with a sigh of relief. She could see Andy's rounded cheeks jutting out from the covers, flushed by the soft pink glow of the night light. As always, just looking at her son was enough to renew her self-confidence. Whatever Morgan thought of her, however he behaved toward her, she decided, she owed it to her child to stay at Kent House and fight for his birthright. She had been running away for much too long.

Chapter Six

THE KENT FAMILY LAWYERS carried on their law practice
in a prestigious section of downtown Boston. Their
names were inscribed on a brass plaque affixed to a solid
mahogany door, but the sign was so small that a casual
passerby might miss it altogether. Clearly, the partners
of Hodge, Trimmer and Barnes felt no need to advertise
their services.

Brooke pushed open the forbidding double doors and
found herself in a paneled, thickly carpeted lobby.

"May I help you?" an elderly secretary asked Brooke
courteously, looking up from her typewriter.

"I'm Mrs. Kent." Strange how difficult it was to claim
that relationship with Morgan. "I have an appointment
with Mr. Barnes."

"Yes, of course, Mrs. Kent. He's been looking forward to seeing you. Please follow me."

Mr. Barnes had an office as dignified and opulent as
the entrance lobby. But he was nothing like the elderly,

white-haired gentleman Brooke had pictured. Tall and thin, he was conservatively dressed in a dark business suit, but his hair was unmistakably red, and his smile was warm as well as polite when he welcomed Brooke into his room.

"I was very sorry to hear of Andrew's death," he said as soon as the secretary had left them alone. "He was a friend of mine as well as a client."

"He was my friend, too," Brooke said, and for the first time in her life she felt that her relationship with Andrew had been placed in proper perspective. Andrew had been her friend. Nothing more and nothing less. She should not allow her memories of their times together to be clouded by other people's anger and suspicions.

"I realize this must be a painful interview for you, Mrs. Kent, so I'll try to keep the conversation as brief and to the point as possible." Mr. Barnes might have red hair and a youthful appearance, but his voice carried the authority of a man who was entirely confident in his role and sure of his professional competence. "Andrew Kent's will was a reasonably simple document, considering the sums of money involved. He left his personal possessions to his brother, Morgan, and to his stepsister, Sheila. He left all his cash assets to the University of New Hampshire, in order to fund a scholarship for inner-city children. And he left his stock in Kent Industries to you, Mrs. Kent. Unconditionally."

Before meeting Mr. Barnes, Brooke had not planned to confide any details of her personal situation to him. Faced with his friendly manner, she decided to risk taking him partially into her confidence.

"You may know, Mr. Barnes, that my husband and I have been . . . estranged . . . for some time."

He acknowledged her words with a fractional nod of his head.

"In many ways I feel unjustified in accepting this

inheritance," she said, twisting her hands nervously together in her lap. She became aware of what she was doing and deliberately held them still. "Perhaps you know I have a young son," she continued. "He's not yet two years old, and I would like to be able to provide for his future. Andrew didn't know about Andy...about my son...but if he had known, I feel confident he would have left his shares in trust for Andy. Under the circumstances, Mr. Barnes, I've decided to accept the legacy."

She looked up at him anxiously and realized that subconsciously she was asking for his approval of her decision. She was relieved—more relieved than she cared to admit—when she found that Mr. Barnes continued to look at her with a friendly smile.

"Mrs. Kent, you don't have to feel guilty about accepting this legacy. Andrew wanted you to have these shares, and that—in law—is all that matters. Your relationship with other members of the Kent family has nothing at all to do with Andrew's right to dispose of his property in any way he saw fit. The shares are yours, Mrs. Kent."

"In that case, I think I should like to sell them right away and establish a trust fund for my son," she said.

Mr. Barnes tipped back his chair and looked at her in silence for a minute. "Has Morgan talked to you about Kent Industries?" he asked at last.

Brooke flushed. "We...we haven't discussed it in detail," she said. Even with this sympathetic man she wasn't prepared to reveal what most of her conversations with Morgan were really like. "He did mention that he was particularly busy at the moment because of some sort of takeover bid."

"You're not a computer expert yourself, Mrs. Kent?"

"No. Have I given myself away already?" She managed a faint smile. "I was trained as an art historian. If you need to know about the influence of the Reformation on sixteenth-century religious painting, I'm just the person you should call."

He returned her smile. "I'll keep that in mind next time the question comes up." He cleared his throat somewhat uncomfortably. "Mrs. Kent, as a lawyer I can only repeat that you are at perfect liberty to do whatever you wish with this inheritance. But knowing the company and Morgan as well as I do, I feel I should explain to you that selling your shares at this precise time would be a grave disservice to Kent Industries."

"Because of the takeover bid?"

"Yes. Kent Industries went public about six years ago. Morgan offered sixty percent of the voting stock in his company to the public and it was snapped up. Kent Industries isn't a giant corporation, but it's known as one of the most innovative and technologically advanced companies involved in the production of microchips and semiconductors. It's large enough to invest heavily in expensive research equipment, but small enough to attract the sort of brilliant young scientist who could easily make the next important breakthrough in computer technology."

"What has all this got to do with selling my shares?"

"The takeover bid is being made by a giant multinational conglomerate headed by a Japanese trading house that has interests in many industries. The conglomerate probably has the financial power to force the deal through if any major shareholder decides to sell out. But, in the opinion of many expert brokers, it doesn't have the management skills to profit from the takeover once it's been made."

"Would Morgan lose a lot of money if the takeover bid is successful?"

"On the contrary. Morgan owns sixteen percent of the shares, and he would make a substantial profit if he sold out at the price the conglomerate is offering. It's the company itself that would suffer, not Morgan personally."

"I see. But why are my shares so important? Eight percent of the stock doesn't seem very much to me."

"You really aren't trained as a businesswoman, are you?" Mr. Barnes's smile remained friendly, and there was no trace of condescension in his voice. "In a takeover attempt," he explained patiently, "control of forty percent of the shares by any one person or organization is normally enough to gain control of the whole company. Your shares represent one-fifth of that amount. Believe me, in such a closely held company your eight-percent holding is extremely significant. In certain circumstances it could be crucial."

"I see. Does anybody else own as much stock as I do?"

"Mr. Kent senior provided the original capital when Morgan started the company twelve years ago, and he still owns some stock. Sheila Kent owns eight percent, the same amount as you. She inherited the shares from her mother."

"Morgan has definitely told you that he doesn't want me to sell my shares?"

Mr. Barnes looked at her sharply, aware of some subtle undertone she hadn't quite managed to eliminate from her voice. The smile faded from his friendly features. "If you insist upon selling your shares, Mrs. Kent, Morgan has authorized me to say that he would like you to sell them directly to him. He will match the offer being made by the conglomerate. However, because of the amount of money involved, he would have to pay you the cash over a period of five years. He would, of course, pay you interest at the current rate."

"Of course," Brooke murmured, then blushed again under Mr. Barnes's shrewd scrutiny. She dropped her gaze so that the lawyer wouldn't be able to see the sudden blaze of triumph that darkened her eyes. In her wildest dreams she had never hoped to possess such a powerful weapon to use against Morgan. If he ever again threatened to fight for custody of Andy, she would know exactly what to say.

"Mrs. Kent?" Mr. Barnes's polite inquiry brought her back to the present. "Have you reached a decision as to what you would like to do?"

"No, I'm afraid I haven't, Mr. Barnes." Brooke was amazed at how cool she managed to keep her voice. "There are several factors for me to take into account. I'm sure you'll understand that this isn't something I can decide in five minutes."

"Perhaps not. But Morgan's offer is a very fair one, Mrs. Kent."

"I'm sure it is. However, if you don't mind, I think I should discuss the matter further . . . with Morgan, you know."

"As you wish." Mr. Barnes rose to his feet and politely escorted Brooke to the door. Even though he showed her every courtesy, Brooke was aware that the warmth had entirely left him. Mr. Barnes was no fool. She had told him herself that she was estranged from Morgan, and he didn't need to be a genius to leap to the conclusion that she intended to use the shares as a weapon in some private battle with her husband.

She reflected that Mr. Barnes was too nice a man to deceive, and she was tempted to reassure him that she would never do anything to undercut Morgan's control of Kent Industries. Whatever her feelings toward her husband—and, God knew, they varied from moment to moment so that she scarcely knew herself what she was feeling—Kent Industries was Morgan's creation and she had no right to interfere in his running of the company. But the lawyer was Morgan's friend, and she wasn't prepared to risk telling him the truth. If the lawyer knew she would never sell her shares, it would take away the only weapon she possessed to protect herself from Morgan.

She almost regretted her decision to remain silent when they reached the outer door of the office. She shook Mr. Barnes's hand, noticing his firm clasp and direct look. Don't worry, she wanted to say. Those shares are safe with me.

Instead, she smiled the remote, impersonal smile she had perfected while working for Tony. "Thank you for your time and your clear explanations, Mr. Barnes. I'll be in touch with you when I reach a decision."

"Thank you, Mrs. Kent." He swung away from her, then paused halfway across the lobby. "Kent Industries employs more than a thousand people," he said. "You will think of them when you make your decision, won't you?"

A faint flush crept into her cheeks. "I'll think about them," she said and hurried out of the office.

Brooke was perched on the edge of the bathtub, watching Andy play with his new floating turtle, when she became aware of Morgan's entry into the bathroom. She pretended not to see him and scooped up a mound of bubbles to put on top of Andy's head. She needed a few seconds to regain control of her racing pulse and erratic heartbeat.

"Dadda!" Andy exclaimed, smacking the bubbles with a hefty thump. Water sprayed out of the tub, drenching Brooke's jeans, and she turned around quickly, unable to ignore Morgan's presence any longer.

"Hello," she said, pleased that the dancing butterfly wings in her stomach didn't seem to be affecting the smoothness of her voice. "Did you have a good day at the office?" She said the first thing that came into her head, only afterward thinking that once again they looked and sounded like a parody of the happy young family.

"It was busy," he replied. "Too many telephone calls, too many meetings, too many hasty decisions. A pretty standard day, I guess." He turned toward the tub, and his mouth relaxed into a faint grin.

"Hi, Andy! What have you got there?"

Andy didn't answer with words. He responded with a little shout of pleasure and a swoosh from one end of the bath to the other. A wave of soapy water cascaded from the tub onto the carpeted floor and sprayed over Morgan's elegant gray business suit.

"Andy, stop that!" Brooke commanded sharply. "You've been told not to slide like that, it's dangerous. Now you'll have to come out of the water." She threw a quick, apologetic glance at Morgan. "I'm sorry. Has he soaked your clothes?"

"It's okay." Morgan rubbed a towel over his pants. He didn't seem annoyed, and Brooke was relieved. Despite the pointlessness of such daydreams, she badly wanted Morgan to approve of the way she had raised her son.

She lifted Andy from the tub, wrapping him in a big, fluffy towel. He wriggled, but in rather a subdued fashion, as if aware that he was in disgrace. Morgan watched them both silently. His manner was remote, but Brooke could have sworn his stern features hovered on the brink of a smile. Her heart gave another little jump when she realized that he must have come straight to her room on returning from the office. Why, she wondered, was Morgan so anxious to see her?

She thought of the unwelcome answer to her own question soon enough. Of course! He wanted to hear right away about her meeting with the lawyers. He wanted to know what she was planning to do with her shares.

"I saw Mr. Barnes this afternoon," she said.

"What did you think of him?" Morgan asked conversationally.

"He . . . he seemed nice."

"He is. And a competent lawyer, too. One of the best around, in fact."

Brooke continued to dry Andy, waiting for Morgan to start questioning her, but he said nothing. Perhaps he didn't need to ask any questions, she thought, as she smoothed baby lotion over Andy's back. The lawyer probably telephoned Morgan with a detailed report as soon as she left the office. Or would that be unethical, a breach of the legal code of professional standards?

She carried Andy through to the bedroom and started to put on his clean pajamas. She heard Morgan let the water out of the tub and realized he was cleaning up the bathroom. She could hardly believe it. Morgan had always had very definite ideas about appropriate roles for men and women, and tidying up bathrooms fell smack into his category of "woman's work."

"Is it Andy's bedtime?" Morgan came into the bedroom just as she closed the last snap on the child's pajamas.

"No, he hasn't eaten dinner yet."

"Would you and Andy like to have dinner with me?"

"With you? You mean, take Andy out to a restaurant? Aren't you planning to eat dinner with your father and Sheila?"

"No, we don't often have family dinners anymore, and I wasn't planning to eat out. I've had our . . . my rooms renovated since you left, and I have my own kitchen now. My fridge is well stocked, and I wondered if you might like to cook dinner for the three of us in my apartment."

She was stunned by his invitation. She brushed Andy's hair, carefully smoothing its silver fairness so that she had an excuse to avoid Morgan's eyes. He must know what she was thinking. How often during their marriage had she complained about their lack of privacy, pleading with Morgan to turn his barnlike two rooms into a small, self-contained apartment. "I feel as though we're living on a movie set," she had once said angrily as they prepared for yet another formal family dinner.

"I'd enjoy cooking dinner," she said finally, putting down the soft hairbrush and letting Andy clamber off the bed. Until she had actually spoken the words of acceptance, she had thought she was going to refuse.

"Good. I'm going to change into something more comfortable and less wet. Come along as soon as you're ready."

"Shall I let the housekeeper know I won't be eating with the rest of the family?" Brooke asked.

"I'll see to it," Morgan said briefly. As he started to walk from the room, Andy called out, "Bye Dadda!"

Morgan paused in the doorway, an indecipherable emotion frozen on his face. "Bye, Andy," he said at last. "See you very soon."

Chapter Seven

AFTER MORGAN HAD GONE, Brooke changed into a pair of peacock-green cords and a paler green cotton shirt. She was only changing because her jeans were a bit damp, she told her reflection in the mirror, but her violet eyes stared back at her accusingly, mocking the lie. She shook her long chestnut-brown hair out of its confining clips and brushed a coral lip gloss onto her mouth with fingers that shook slightly. She stared at her reflection for a moment, then snatched a tissue and scrubbed all the lipstick off.

"Come on, Andy," she said, grabbing his hand. "It's time to go eat dinner."

The door to Morgan's rooms stood open, and she entered without knocking, hovering uncertainly on the threshold as she rapidly inventoried the many changes that had been made since she ran away from Kent House.

The original sitting room had been converted into an open living area. A kitchen and eating section was separated from the rest of the room by a long counter with a built-in bar at one end. The large, old-fashioned fireplace remained, but it was now flanked by two new, comfortable-looking armchairs. Multicolored floor cushions were scattered on the thick carpet, close to the hearth. The drapes, closed to shut out the darkness, were a deep russet color. The warm cherry wood of the kitchen cabinets added to the general feeling of relaxed comfort.

Morgan stood behind the counter, opening a bottle of wine, but he put it in an ice bucket at the sound of her arrival, crossing the room swiftly and closing the door for her. Suddenly his apartment seemed very isolated from the rest of the house—and very quiet.

"Welcome back," Morgan said, breaking the silence. "I've . . . missed you."

Her heart started to hammer erratically. "I like the changes you've made," she said, trying to sound casual. "You've created an attractive apartment."

"I'm glad you like it."

"Hi Dadda!" Andy had completed a quick tour of inspection and seemed to like the room. Having bounced twice on a fat cushion, he returned to his mother's side. "Play?" he asked hopefully, staring up at Morgan.

"Okay, we'll play while Mom cooks." Morgan ruffled Andy's hair. "Look on the chair. There's a box with something inside."

"Cat?" Andy asked, his eyes lighting up with anticipation.

Morgan was laughing as he looked at Brooke. "That damn cat! I wish the housekeeper had never let it into the house. It's supposed to be a barn animal, you know."

"I take it that the box on the chair doesn't contain a kitten?" Brooke laughed in reply.

"No, nothing so exciting. It's a wooden train. When I bought it this afternoon, I thought it would be a real favorite. Now I'm not so sure . . . in comparison with a cat."

"I'll start the meal," Brooke said. "I think you'd better rescue the box before it falls on the floor. Andy's not too good at unwrapping packages."

Morgan did as she suggested, then squatted down on the carpet next to Andy as they pushed the train on a long journey around the living room floor. Brooke hummed softly under her breath as she finally turned her attention to the kitchen cabinets in order to decide what to prepare for dinner.

She had become expert at cooking interesting meals quickly. Her work at Tony's hadn't left her with time to spare for making dinners that required hours of chopping and slicing, followed by hours of pot watching. Within a few minutes she had decided on a menu, using the chicken breasts Morgan had already placed on the counter to thaw. She brushed the chicken lightly with butter and seasoned it with paprika and fresh green peppers before putting it into the oven to bake. While it was cooking, she prepared some rice and tossed a salad in a dressing made from lemon juice, tarragon, and oil. In forty-five minutes the meal was ready and the table elegantly set. She wedged one of the floor cushions into a chair for Andy as she called out that dinner was served.

Morgan unclasped Andy from his back, standing upright with a heartfelt groan of relief. "Thank goodness," he said. "Five more minutes of being a horse, and I might not have survived to appreciate the food."

Andy was jumping up and down, too excited to speak. His words tumbled over one another in a stream of garbled sound. Brooke set the salad bowl on the table with a distinct thud.

"Come and sit down, Andy," she ordered, more sharply than she had intended. She saw Morgan's look of inquiry and attempted a smile without much success. Her stomach had started to churn with a volatile mixture of happiness and anxiety. The whole evening was beginning to incorporate too many of her secret fantasies. The laden table, the flicker of warm firelight, and the smiling faces of her husband and her son were all images plucked straight out of her subconscious yearnings.

But Morgan would never play the domesticated family man on a permanent basis, she reminded herself. He had probably planned tonight for a special reason, hoping to talk Brooke out of selling her shares. Once he had his guarantee, he would revert to his old style, staying out at the office until all hours of the night, expecting Brooke to wait patiently at home twiddling her thumbs while the servants did all the work.

"Let's sit down, shall we?" she asked sharply, not liking the trend of her own thoughts. She pushed Andy's chair close to the table, then cut a portion of chicken into tiny pieces, putting them on Andy's plate with a spoonful of rice. She gave Andy a spoon, then sat down, trying to avoid Morgan's gaze. He looked so friendly and relaxed that she had to fight against the dangerous impulse to let down her defenses and smile back at him.

Morgan sniffed appreciatively at the steaming platter of chicken. "Everything smells terrific and looks even better," he said. He helped himself to generous portions from each dish on the table, then stood up to fetch the bottle of wine from the counter. He poured some of the sparkling Rhine wine into their glasses before lifting his drink in a quick salute.

"Thank you for making dinner tonight. I needed some time away from everybody so that I could just relax. It's been a hell of a day."

"It was my pleasure," Brooke said stiffly. Why had he found it a hell of a day? she wondered. Had Mr. Barnes told him that his wife was going to sell her shares, leaving him vulnerable to takeover by the conglomerate? Once again she waited for him to start asking the questions she dreaded, but he seemed to have no interest in finding out the details of her conversation with the lawyer.

"Have you seen the exhibition of French medieval painting at the museum?" he asked as they started to eat.

"Yes. I went one Sunday with Andy. He's getting quite accustomed to being pushed around museums and picture galleries. I often wonder what he thinks I'm doing, because all he can see from his stroller must be people's knees!"

Morgan laughed. "It's a tough life, being a baby. So what did you think of the miniatures by Jean Fouquet?"

She was startled by his familiarity with the exhibition, but not wanting to bore him she kept her answer short. Almost without her being aware of it, he encouraged her to expand her brief response, and soon they were involved in one of the rambling, exciting discussions that had filled the early days of their relationship. Brooke realized she was hungry for this sort of intellectual stimulation. It had been too long since she last allowed herself the luxury of a truly adult conversation.

"All gone!" Andy's words brought her down to earth with a thump. He had finished his meal and was busily engaged in banging his spoon on the empty plate. Since the plate was fine bone china instead of the plastic he was used to, the spoon was producing a loud ringing noise that he obviously found fascinating.

"That's enough, Andy." Morgan removed the spoon at the same moment that Brooke reached for it, and for a moment her hand went quite still. Then she snatched her fingers away from the unexpected contact.

"I'll get a paper towel for Andy," she said hurriedly. "These paper napkins tend to shred." She needed some excuse to walk away from the table. Morgan had merely touched her, and her whole body had seemed to spring into sudden, vibrant life. In two years of working at Tony's she had never met another man who had elicited any physical response at all. She ripped a paper towel from the roll, dampened it with hot water, and forced her emotions back under control.

"He's almost asleep," she said as she wiped Andy's mouth and hands. "I think I'd better go back to my room and put him to bed." She started to lift the sleepy toddler out of his chair, pleased to have an excuse to escape from Morgan's apartment. She had enjoyed the meal and enjoyed their conversation. Too much, in fact. Now it was time to clamp down on her physical awareness and get their relationship back on a less intimate foundation.

"Andy can sleep on the floor," Morgan said. "Look, we'll pile the floor cushions around him. He's almost asleep, so there shouldn't be any problem."

"It would be more sensible to put him in his crib," she said.

"But what about my dessert? Don't you remember my fatal sweet tooth?"

Brooke remembered no such thing. She wanted to protest, but Morgan took Andy from her arms and carried him purposefully across the room. He disappeared into his bedroom for a moment and emerged carrying a soft travel blanket and a pillow. He quickly spread the blanket over the floor and piled floor cushions around it. He placed Andy on the blanket, tucking the teddy bear and Andy's own blue security blanket between the half-sleeping child and the pile of cushions.

"Good night, Andy," he said softly.

Andy didn't bother to remove his thumb from his mouth. "Nigh' Dadda," he mumbled.

Brooke knelt and gave her son a kiss, still not sure she was doing the sensible thing in agreeing to spend more time alone with Morgan.

Andy removed his thumb and gave her an unexpected hug. His wet thumb brushed her cheek. "Night Momma."

"Night," she whispered.

"Let's eat dessert," Morgan said, moving briskly away from Andy's makeshift bed. He walked round the room switching off lamps until only the kitchen light remained.

"I imagine Andy will sleep better if it's not so bright," he said.

"Yes." Brooke cleared her throat, determined to sound as casual as Morgan did. She refused to notice how the dim light softened the harsh angles of Morgan's face, emphasizing the lines of weariness and leaving an impression of unusual vulnerability.

"I thought we could have cherries jubilee for dessert," she said. "You have some vanilla ice cream in the freezer, and I found a can of black cherries in one of the cupboards."

"Sounds great. That was a super chicken recipe, Brooke. I've done a lot of my own cooking over the past year, but I'm still pretty much in the stage of opening frozen packages and following the directions." As he was speaking, Morgan carried the remaining dishes from the table and helped Brooke stack them in the dishwasher.

"Even that's a great improvement over the way you were when we were first married. I swear, you couldn't boil a kettle of water!"

Morgan laughed openly. "Listen to who's talking. Do you remember the first meal you cooked for me? I don't think I've ever met anyone else who actually managed to burn an entire pan of noodles. I mean really burn them until they were black!"

"Yes, I have to admit that was quite a meal," Brooke agreed with a tiny laugh. "I think those noodles smelled even worse than they looked!"

"I certainly wasn't expecting lumpy tomato sauce and burned spaghetti when I dashed out of my lecture to offer you a ride home!"

"No," she said dryly. "I'm sure you weren't. From the way you came on to me, I never did think food was at the forefront of your mind."

Morgan's eyes danced with fresh amusement. "What's a guy supposed to think when some beautiful, unknown female turns up in his advanced computer class and sits in the front row, fluttering her eyelashes? Especially since it was obvious within thirty seconds of your arrival that you didn't know a binary code from a semiconductor!"

"I came into your class by mistake, you know that," Brooke protested demurely. "I've explained a hundred times that there was an unexpected change of classrooms. I was supposed to be in a graduate history class on the theology of the Reformation!"

"That's your story," Morgan murmured. "How come, if you were expecting a class in theology, you sat through forty-five minutes of my lecture on ferrite cores in computer memory systems?"

"I guess you must be a brilliant lecturer," Brooke said airily. Her gaze locked inadvertently with Morgan's, and a rush of heated color stained her cheeks. "The cherries are hot now," she said hastily. "Have you got some cognac so we can flame them?"

Morgan ignored her question. He put his hand beneath her chin, turning her around very slowly. "I gave the worst lecture of my career that afternoon," he said. "I couldn't take my eyes off you. I thought you were the sexiest woman any man could ever hope to find." He paused for a moment before adding, "But I was wrong."

She was aware of a knife edge of pain cutting through her body, and she dropped her lashes quickly to hide the hurt in her eyes. Through the darkness she sensed Morgan's head bending over her, then his lips brushed her mouth in an agonizingly sweet and fleeting caress.

"I was definitely wrong," he said. "Three years ago you were desirable, but now you're absolutely stunning."

For a blissful moment she let herself relax against the

hard strength of his body. He wanted her, she realized with a primitive shock of pleasure, and he didn't care if she knew it. His hands pressed her hips more tightly against him, and she jerked away in panic.

He didn't attempt to restrain her. He dropped his hands to his side and reached casually into a nearby cupboard. "The best brandy," he said, pouring a generous measure into the cherries, which were bubbling ominously on the burner. "Only the best for your gourmet cooking, my dear." He lit a match and held it over the surface of the pot. It exploded into flames, and Brooke watched the dancing blue fire until it died away completely. It was easier to look at the cherries than to face up to the reality of the way her body was still feeling.

They ate their dessert quickly, without saying much, and Brooke sprang up as soon as she had swallowed the last mouthful. "Thanks for a delicious meal, Morgan. I'll make you some coffee if you like, but Andy and I really ought to be going."

Unhurriedly, Morgan got up and pulled her to his side, stilling her agitated and ineffectual movements. "Stop pretending," he said huskily. "Andy's fast asleep, so if you go it will be because you want to. Do you want to leave me, Brooke?"

She tried to say yes, but her vocal chords wouldn't obey the rational commands of her brain. For a few fatal seconds she said nothing at all while his hands gently caressed the length of her spine. Then his lips covered hers in a sudden, urgent kiss, and it was immediately too late to talk about leaving. Her body had betrayed her.

"Come and sit by the fire," Morgan murmured.

Brooke found her voice at last. "Andy..." she said in a feeble protest.

"He only has one side of the fire. We can take the other."

Morgan flipped off the kitchen light so casually that

Brooke was scarcely aware of his action. He pulled her down on the pile of cushions in front of the fire, cradling her head against his arm. They seemed wrapped in a warm and velvet darkness.

Brooke welcomed the dark. Under its obscuring cover she could acknowledge feelings she would never allow herself to admit in the harsh light of day.

Andy made a small, snuffling sound as Brooke stretched out her legs toward the fire. Morgan leaned over and gently pushed Andy's teddy bear back into the crook of his arm. Brooke noticed how the firelight tinted their hair with an identical shade of burnished copper, and her heart ached with a deep and only half-understood yearning.

"He's a beautiful baby," Morgan said as Andy settled back into a deep sleep.

"I think so, too." Brooke's mouth quirked into a smile. "Of course, since I'm his mother I suppose some people might say I'm prejudiced."

Morgan traced the outline of her smile in a brief, delicate caress. "Some people would be wrong," he said softly. "You've done a fantastic job of raising him, Brooke. His nature seems as full of sunshine as his looks."

Silence fell between them, broken only by the collapse of a log into the grate, which died in a shower of burning embers. "I wish he were my son," Morgan said so quietly that Brooke wasn't sure if she imagined the faint, hesitant question that inflected his words.

She was surprised to find that for the first time she felt no anger at Morgan's doubts, only sadness. Perhaps, she conceded, he had good reasons for his uncertainty. By the time Andy was conceived, their marriage had passed from a stage of stormy turmoil and passionate reconciliation to a frozen wasteland of icy silences and unspoken recrimination. Small wonder, she thought, that Morgan preferred not to remember the one turbulent night of sexual rage when he had forced himself on her and Andy had been conceived.

"You've never believed me in the past, Morgan," she said at last. "Would you believe me now if I told you that Andy is your son?"

It seemed to Brooke that he was silent for an eternity before he turned to her with a groan of frustration. "Oh hell, Brooke, I don't want to talk about the past. Not now, not when I have you here in my arms."

She turned away, feeling angry, but he nudged her head around and covered her mouth with his in a fierce, hungry kiss. His hands held her tightly against his body, making her fully aware of his arousal.

She wanted to resist. It was humiliating to find that she still craved the lovemaking of a man who didn't trust her, but Morgan slowly pushed up her sweater and, when she felt the heat of his breath against her skin, her resistance vanished. His tongue stroked the hollow between her breasts, and her body gave an immediate, involuntary shudder.

"It was always like this between us," Morgan said huskily. "Do you remember how it was when we made love, Brooke?"

"I remember," she whispered. "I wanted to forget but I couldn't, however hard I tried."

"You never used to wear a bra," Morgan said as his fingers expertly unfastened the tiny front hook.

She didn't reply because it was impossible to form coherent sentences when his tongue was roaming over her naked breasts, creating little streaks of fire wherever it passed. She found the buttons on his shirt and undid them one by one, caressing him with trembling hands as she did so. She rubbed her cheek against the coarse, wiry hair of his chest, and it seemed that two years of loneliness were soothed away by the touch of his rough hair against her skin.

Very gently, Morgan lifted her face, framing it in his

hands so that he could kiss her again. His mouth fluttered tiny kisses against her eyelids and, when his tongue finally pushed against her lips, she welcomed the invasion, arching her body so that the hair on his chest brushed against her breasts, teasing them into awareness. With tantalizing slowness, Morgan stroked the hardened nipples, and her desire sharpened into acute, painful need.

He felt the new urgency of her response, and his mouth covered hers with an insatiable, drowning hunger. Brooke caught her breath in a gasp of panic, but she returned his kiss. Very soon, she realized, the demands of her body would take over completely, and she would be begging Morgan to consummate their lovemaking. She had been starving for the touch of his body for so long, and now she ached to experience the fulfillment of their union. Her body was already dissolving into a mass of dissonant nerve endings that would only become whole again at the moment of Morgan's possession.

She ran her fingers down the hard length of his spine, reveling in the feel of bone and firm muscle. It was so much more satisfactory in reality than in the clouded memories of her dreams. "Morgan . . ." she said, not sure whether she was begging him to stop or continue. "Morgan . . . please . . ."

"Don't talk," he ordered. "Don't say anything." His breathing was sharp and shallow, and his hands shook with need as he stroked her thighs, but his words produced a sudden, tiny chill on the edges of Brooke's passion-clouded brain. Her pulses continued to pound with an insistent, throbbing rhythm, but her heart felt suddenly cold. "Why can't I speak, Morgan?" she asked.

He hesitated for a fraction of a second. "Because I want to kiss you," he said.

She made no protest when he suited his action to his words. She lay passively against the cushions, but failed to respond to the touch of his lips against her own.

"What is it?" Morgan asked finally.

She sat up, avoiding his gaze as she pulled her sweater back on. She wanted to get dressed while she had the chance, because she carried no illusions as to how long she could hold out against Morgan's lovemaking if he really tried to seduce her.

"It's no use," she said despairingly. "We can't use sex as if it were a drug that keeps us too intoxicated to face up to reality. We can't build a worthwhile relationship on silent sex."

Morgan ran impatient fingers through his hair, then pushed his shirt into the waistband of his trousers. "You're way ahead of me, Brooke. I didn't know we were trying to build a new relationship. Frankly, I hadn't moved past the thought of enjoying the pleasures of your body."

"I can't make love to a man who doesn't trust me! Do you realize that just now you were afraid to let me speak because you assumed that anything I said—anything at all—was likely to destroy our temporary harmony. That doesn't say much for our relationship, does it?" She lowered her voice, turning away so she wouldn't have to meet his suddenly cold expression. "I don't need your lovemaking quite that badly, Morgan."

"Don't you? Personally, I'm prepared to trade in quite a few of my moral principles to possess your highly desirable body." His eyes blazed with a passion that mocked the calmness of his voice, and she drew in a quick, shallow breath.

"Don't you understand, Morgan? That's precisely the problem!" She hurriedly stepped out of the circle of firelight, aware that she hovered no more than a hair's breadth away from throwing caution to the winds. One touch, one gentle word, and she was likely to end up in his arms.

"I have to go," she said desperately. "I think Andy is about to wake up."

Morgan looked at the sleeping baby. "Sure," he said

sarcastically. "I can see that he's crying out for his crib."

He watched in tense silence as Brooke hastily gathered Andy into her arms, wrapping the blanket round his sturdy body.

"G-goodnight, Morgan. Thanks for dinner... and everything."

He opened the door of his apartment, and for a moment their eyes met over Andy's sleeping form. "Run away if you feel you have to," he said softly. "Let me know when you finally decide to stop running."

Chapter Eight

BROOKE THRUST HER HANDS deep into the pockets of her knitted jacket. It was a brilliantly sunny morning, but the chill of a New England fall frosted the clear air. She watched with a smile as her son staggered around the neatly cut lawn, clutching a beach ball that was almost as big as he was. Mr. Kent was pretending to chase Andy, growling out threats as he claimed possession of the ball. Andy's shrieks of excitement rang across the formal gardens, bouncing off the imposing stone walls of Kent House.

Brooke's smile contained a hint of anxiety as she turned to speak to the nurse. "My father-in-law won't exhaust himself, will he?" she asked in a low voice. "He looks so frail."

"Moderate exercise is good for him," Angela said. "It's Andy who's doing all the running, anyway. Mr. Kent is a veteran parent who knows how to make a little energy go a long way."

"Having an active toddler around certainly should make him appreciate the benefits of an afternoon nap!" Brooke replied.

Angela smiled her agreement. "I'll go and join them for a little while," she said. "That way Mr. Kent can take a breather if he needs it. Are you coming, too?"

"No, I think Andy has enough doting adults playing with him already. He'll soon be so spoiled he'll be unbearable. If you don't need me for a few minutes, I'll grab a cup of coffee."

Angela nodded cheerfully. "See you later."

Brooke strolled toward the house, pausing every now and then to watch the noisy game in progress on the lawn. She saw Mr. Kent change his tactics and begin throwing the ball to Andy, who had no idea how to catch anything so huge. Each time the beach ball hit his tummy, Andy collapsed on the grass with a loud squeal of delight. Angela's role in the new game seemed to be to persuade Andy to stop rolling around on the ground long enough to throw the ball back to his grandfather. Her son, Brooke decided wryly, didn't look as if had the natural instincts of an all-star pitcher.

A faint shadow fell across the gravel path, cutting off some of the warmth of the sun. Brooke looked up and saw her stepsister-in-law standing in front of her. She forced herself to smile, even though she had secretly hoped to see Morgan.

"Hello, Sheila," she said politely.

"Good morning." Sheila hesitated a moment. "They're having fun, aren't they?" she said, gesturing toward the boisterous trio.

"Yes." An unwelcome spark of honesty compelled Brooke to add, "Andy loves all the grass and open space. We were . . . very cramped in our Boston apartment."

"Andy is just the tonic my father needed, as I'm sure you can see." Sheila kicked at a flat white stone on the gravel path. "I'm . . . er . . . glad you came back, Brooke. I hope . . . I hope you'll stay for a while."

Brooke forced herself to look directly into Sheila's eyes. "Do you mean that?" she asked. "Do you really hope that we'll stay? If so, I'm amazed at the change. You certainly didn't want me here two years ago."

Sheila's eyes faltered, fluttering away before coming to rest determinedly on the stones at her feet. "I was only nineteen when you married Morgan," she said. "You came into our lives and immediately the whole house seemed turned upside down to welcome you. My father thought you were wonderful, Andrew was halfway toward being in love with you, and Morgan . . ."

"And Morgan?" Brooke prompted gently when Sheila's words tailed into silence.

"Morgan just about worshipped the ground you walked on. You know that. And you knew I was in love with him, didn't you?"

"Yes."

Sheila pushed her hair out of her eyes with an impatient gesture.

"I felt like such a fool, falling in love with my own stepbrother. Looking back on it, I can see it was probably nothing more than a teenage crush, but it took me a long time to get over it."

"Are you sure you're over it now?" Brooke asked.

"Yes. I'm not in love with Morgan any more. I've accepted the fact that my stepbrother is a one-woman man, and I know I'm never going to be that woman. And I really don't care anymore, Brooke. In fact, I'm going to get married myself. I've met somebody who's pretty special to me."

"Congratulations, I'm very happy for you! Is it someone I know?" Brooke was surprised to find that her friendly words were actually sincere.

"No. David's an engineer from New York. I met him

while I was taking a computer-science course at Columbia. Perhaps you'd like to have dinner with us some time."

"Why, yes, thank you, I would."

"Well, this isn't exactly why I came outside to find you. I owe you an apology, Brooke, and I also want to ask for your help."

"I was about to go inside to get some coffee," Brooke said. "Do you want to join me? If *you're* going to ask *me* for help, I think I may need to be sitting down!"

Sheila's laugh sounded a little nervous. "The apology is quite short," she said as they walked together toward the side entrance to the house. "I was devastated by the news of Andrew's death, and I didn't react very well when Morgan told us he'd found out where you were hiding and that he was bringing you back to Rendford. I suppose the news that you were coming back was just one problem too many on top of all the other shocks we'd had. I didn't seem able to cope with the fact that you had a son. Andy is a beautiful baby, and I think I was jealous. I was thoroughly unpleasant when you arrived, and I'm sorry."

"A mother will forgive anything if a person tells her often enough that her baby is beautiful." Brooke spoke casually, attempting to lighten Sheila's self-accusing mood. "And of course I understand that everybody here has been under stress because of what happened to Andrew."

"Yes, we've all been under a strain," Sheila agreed. "Would you like me to brew the coffee?" she asked as they entered the house. "The cleaning staff will be working upstairs at this time of day, so we can have the kitchen to ourselves."

"Yes, if you have time." Brooke glanced at her watch. "It's almost ten o'clock. Don't you have to go to the office?"

"Morgan and I are going to New York on the one o'clock shuttle out of Logan Airport, so I have a few minutes. We have meetings scheduled with the company's bankers so that we can make sure our lines of emergency credit are still open."

"Is Morgan... is he home?"

"How can you ask? No, of course he's at the office, but I told him I needed to take a couple of hours off." Sheila slid the glass coffee pot under the filter and plugged in the coffee maker.

"Morgan's changed since you left," she said abruptly. "He always worked hard and he was alway ambitious, but since you went away he's turned into a machine, dedicated to the service of Kent Industries. Sometimes I think he lives, breathes, eats, and sleeps the company."

"I don't see why you consider that a change," Brooke said with unintentional bitterness.

"It's different now," Sheila insisted. "When you were living here Morgan worked hard, but he was sensitive to the human needs and failings of people around him. Now he doesn't seem to notice people anymore except as they relate to Kent Industries."

Brooke paced jerkily across the kitchen floor. "So now he's a full-time machine and before he was only ninety percent computer. Does it make all that much difference?"

"Yes," Sheila said tersely. "I'm worried about my father. Brooke, before this takeover bid came up, my father had decided to sell his shares in Kent Industries and move somewhere warmer. He told me he wanted to live in a small cottage by a big lake and spend his days fishing. Of course he never came right out and told Morgan the truth, and Morgan wouldn't listen to me. Then this threat of a takeover intervened , and Dad won't hear of selling his shares now. Morgan says that he is worried about his father's health, but he doesn't seem to notice that Dad is getting old and tired and doesn't want to talk about finances and stocks and asset bases any more. The business is Morgan's life, and he thinks it ought to be the center of everybody else's life, too. Can you help make him understand that Dad wants to give up all his financial responsibilities and spend some time enjoying his retirement?"

"The coffee's ready," Brooke said, glad of an excuse not to reply immediately. She poured out two steaming mugs, then turned to face her stepsister-in-law. "You've been honest with me," she said at last, "so you deserve an honest answer. Sheila, I have no influence over Morgan's actions and decisions. I would help you if I could, but if you think you're powerless, then I'm even more so."

Sheila's blue eyes slowly darkened with amazement. "You really believe that, don't you? You really think you have no influence on Morgan? My heavens, I can't believe you're so blind! If you told him that the sun rose in the west, I think he'd believe you were telling him the truth."

Brooke's laugh was tinged with hysteria. "If only you knew how far away from the truth you are! Morgan would suspect a double meaning if I told him black was black." She realized how close she was coming to making an admission she didn't intend to make, and she pushed back her chair with a clatter. "I shouldn't have said that," she said as she tossed the dregs of her coffee into the sink.

For just a moment Sheila's mouth twisted into the hard smile Brooke had always dreaded. "I often wondered what caused you two to split up, and I'm beginning to understand at last," Sheila said. She took a thoughtful sip of her coffee and, to Brooke's relief, her expression softened again. "Two years ago I'd have done my best to increase every doubt Morgan had about you," she admitted. "Thank God, I've grown up a bit since then, and I understand myself a whole lot better than I used to. It isn't that Morgan doesn't trust you, Brooke. It's just that he's so unsure of himself where you're concerned."

"Morgan! Unsure of himself? Can we both be talking about the same Morgan Kent? I'm talking about my husband, the arrogant devil who strides through life calmly helping himself to whatever he happens to want."

"Brooke, *you're* the only woman Morgan has ever really wanted, and he's been terrified of losing you, right from the first evening he met you. Think of things from his point of view. He was accustomed to having eligible young women throw themselves into his arms. You didn't do any such thing. Quite the contrary, in fact, from what I gather. Morgan had to do all the chasing."

Brooke's attempt at a sarcastic laugh was somewhat shaky.

"Oh, sure, I presented a real challenge to his legendary charm. I think I managed to keep myself out of his bed for at least two weeks."

"Well, that's about thirteen days longer than he bothered chasing any of his other girlfriends! He once jokingly told Andrew and me that he didn't know how to impress you. Here you were, the one and only woman he'd ever wanted to marry, and you seemed as happy as a clam studying medieval history and sharing a run-down apartment with a bunch of students. Can't you see the irony of the situation? For the first time in his life he wanted to win a woman's favor by casting the world at her feet, and all you wanted to do was to spend your time touring the free exhibitions at the local museums. You seemed to be utterly indifferent to his money, and you told him that you despised computers. He, on the other hand, knew very little about art, which seemed to be your passion. He felt he had nothing to offer you."

"You're wrong. You must be wrong. Morgan must have known I was crazy about him right from the first." Brooke's voice died away to a mere thread of sound. "I told him often enough how much I loved him."

"But did you show him?" Sheila stood up, making no further comment on Brooke's whispered words. "I have to pack a suitcase for New York," she said. "But please think about what I've said. Morgan is a man who will always need the highs that come from business success. He's intensely competitive, and he thrives on challenges and power plays. But he needs you, too, and I think he realizes just how much."

Sheila paused at the kitchen door, her face alight with self-mockery. "Listen to me," she said. "Auntie Sheila's advice to the lovelorn. If Kent Industries gets taken over, perhaps I can start a new career writing advice columns in the local newspaper." She closed the door with a faint bang, and Brooke heard the staccato of her footsteps followed by a distant murmur of voices.

Morgan came into the kitchen before she had finished rinsing out the coffee mugs. The late-morning sun angled in through a high window, burnishing his thick silver-tinged hair. The dark trousers of his business suit clung to his thighs, and he carried the jacket slung over one shoulder. He had unbuttoned his shirt beneath his loosely knotted maroon tie, and Brooke felt her body flame with unwelcome heat.

"I met Sheila," Morgan said. "She told me I could find you here."

Brooke turned back to the sink, drying her hands with painstaking thoroughness before she spoke. "Do you want...would you like some coffee? Sheila just made it."

"No thanks, not right now." He looked swiftly round the kitchen. "Where's Andy?"

"Outside playing with your father and the nurse."

"I see. Would you spare me a couple of minutes, Brooke? If we could go into my study, I have some things to discuss with you."

She followed him reluctantly, sensing that the moment she had been dreading had finally arrived. He was going to ask her about Andrew's shares. They were her shares now, she reminded herself.

Morgan pushed open the door to his study, tossing his briefcase onto a chair and walking behind his desk before turning to face her. Brooke stood nervously in front of the desk, trying to appear unconcerned. She hated this room, which was where Morgan had so often chosen to barricade himself during the last, silent months of their marriage. It was dark and gloomy, with heavy furniture left over from a previous generation crowded into the corners. Even the big windows, shaded by the thick trunks of old oak trees, didn't admit much light. She had never understood why Morgan chose to work here.

"I've spoken to my lawyer," he said abruptly. "He thinks you're planning to sell the Kent Industries shares Andrew left you."

Brooke hesitated. "I'm thinking about it," she said.

"I see." Morgan's glance moved away from hers, out over the rows of trees. He lifted his hand and pressed a couple of fingers to the taut skin between his eyes, then shrugged his shoulders as if to relieve the tension of tight, overstrained muscles. Brooke's heart contracted in sympathy at the weariness conveyed by his unconscious gestures, but she deliberately shut her mind to Morgan's problems. She wasn't obliged to justify herself to him. She owed him nothing. She forced herself to speak calmly.

"I need to establish a trust fund for Andy," she said. "I need to provide for his future with a diversified portfolio of secure investments. Kent Industries is too risky to form the basis of a child's trust fund."

"Can't you wait for a few weeks? That's all I'm asking. My credit lines are stretched almost to the limit. I don't know if I can find the cash to buy up your shares right now, but I can't afford to let them become available on the open market."

She stared down at the floor, working up the willpower to resist Morgan's implicit appeal for her support. She had to remember that her future with Andy was at stake.

"I won't sell my shares in your company," she said. "On one condition."

"Name it."

"That you draw up a watertight legal document permanently renouncing all right to custody of Andy."

Fatigue and every other trace of emotion were wiped from Morgan's face as if by a giant eraser. "So that you can disappear again as soon as it's signed? Is that your plan, Brooke?"

"No!" she said. "Now that I've seen Andy here with y...here with his grandfather, I know I have no right to keep y...them apart."

He was silent. Time seemed to tick by endlessly. "I accept your condition," he said finally.

She let her breath out in a long, low sigh, aware that she ought to feel triumphant. Morgan wasn't going to fight her for custody of Andy, and she had promised him almost nothing in return. But the feeling of triumph didn't come. Instead she had to conquer an overwhelming urge to rest her head against his chest. Suddenly she wanted to soothe away the lines of strain etched into his face, and to feel the faint roughness of his shaven skin under the tips of her fingers.

"I have to leave for New York in twenty minutes," Morgan said, his voice flattened by a restrained emotion that Brooke couldn't interpret. There was an infinitesimal pause before he added, "I'll look forward to seeing you and Andy when I get back."

She felt a curious wrenching in her heart when he spoke. "We'll be waiting," she said, then coughed to clear an inexplicable huskiness in her throat. She found that she was watching Morgan intently as he crossed the room to retrieve his briefcase.

"Good luck with your bankers," she said. "I hope your talks go well."

He looked up, apparently seeing something in her face that she would rather have concealed. He moved with unbelievable swiftness, pulling her into his arms and kissing her with a slow, deep hunger. She was shivering when he finally lifted his head. "That's to remember me by while I'm away," he said harshly. His lean fingers moved from her neck to her lips, gently touching them in a caress that was almost more seductive than a kiss. "You're beautiful," he said.

He picked up his briefcase. The door closed quietly behind him, and Brooke was once more alone in the silent study.

She drove into Boston that same afternoon with the intention of collecting her clothes and some of Andy's baby equipment from her apartment. There were practical matters she needed to attend to if she was going to stay at Kent House for a while.

It was strange to come back to her tiny walk-up after the spaciousness of Kent House. The familiar furniture, the fixtures in the bathroom and the kitchen, all seemed alien to her touch, as if she were no longer the same woman who had left here only a few days ago.

The thought was an uncomfortable one, and she closed the lock on her full suitcase with a decided snap. She walked into the kitchen and dialed Tony's number, faintly relieved to discover when he replied that he sounded exactly the same as he always had—vulgar, cynical, and probably kinder than he wanted anyone to guess.

"I won't be coming to work for you anymore, Tony," she said after their exchange of greetings. "I guess my few days off have extended a bit. I'm going to be a full-time housewife for a while."

"So what else is new? Morgan already told me that, honey. He called me at five in the morning that night he took you home from here. My wife quits, he said, or words to that effect."

Brooke felt a trace of emotion, hard to identify, and covered it quickly with a spurt of genuine annoyance. Damn Morgan with his overbearing assumption that he could walk into her life and order it to his pleasing!

"I'm sorry for the short notice, Tony," she said. "I enjoyed working for you, and I'm really grateful to you, as well. You gave me a job when I needed one."

"Any time, sugar. And if you ever need a job again, think of me." He cut off her thanks in mid-sentence. "Remember, I'll only employ you as long as you keep that gorgeous body. Don't lose your figure living it up with all those fat cats in New Hampshire. Think exercise! Think thin!"

She was still smiling as she hung up the phone and walked slowly down the apartment hallway to knock on Joan Krakowski's door.

"Hi! Can I beg a cup of coffee?" she said as soon as her friend opened the door.

"Brooke, come in! Boy, am I glad to see you! We wondered what happened to you, although your ...er...husband did telephone and ask us to keep an eye on things while you were gone." Joan swept a stuffed rabbit and several plastic cars off the living room sofa. "Sit down, Brooke, and tell me what you've been doing with yourself. The twins and the baby are all asleep at the same time, so it must have been fate that brought you to the door at this precise moment!"

Brooke sank into the comfortably sagging cushions of the sofa. "Oh, it's good to see you again, Joan. You sound just the same as always."

"Why shouldn't I?" Joan's glance at her friend was faintly whimsical. "*I* haven't been running off to New Hampshire with a devastating man who looks as if he just walked off a movie set!"

Brooke could feel color flare in her cheeks. "Morgan...my husband...is a research engineer. He designs computers."

"That may be his job title, honey. But what he is is a six-foot package of sexual dynamite!"

Brooke twisted her hands nervously in her lap. "Yes," she said. "I guess that kind of describes Morgan. Sometimes...sometimes it's not very easy to be married to a package of dynamite."

"Do you want to talk about it?" Joan asked. She gave a little laugh. "Of course, if you say no, I'll probably die of sheer, unsatisfied curiosity!"

"I think maybe I do want to talk about it," Brooke said. "I'm so confused, I don't know what I feel about anything anymore. Maybe you could tell me what I ought to do."

"Putting a problem into words sometimes helps us to see it in a different light," Joan commented. "But I don't want to give you advice. That's a sure way to ruin a beautiful friendship."

Brooke saw the warmth in her friend's eyes and suddenly decided to analyze her relationship with Morgan as honestly as she could. "Morgan and I only knew each other six weeks before we got married," she said. "If it's possible to fall in love at first sight, then that's what we did. We didn't meet each other's families until the night before the wedding ceremony. The way we felt about each other seemed to make families irrelevant." She smiled with a touch of self-mockery. "You could say that I'm now a slightly older and much wiser woman. I realize that you never marry a person in a vacuum, and in Morgan's case his family was more important than most. For a start, he lived with his father and brother and stepsister, and they were all involved in running the family business. We had a two-week honeymoon in a cabin in the New Hampshire mountains, and I thought we'd found paradise. Then we drove back to Kent House, and I came back to reality, with a capital R."

"The family kept interfering?" Joan asked sympathetically.

"Not exactly, not at first. Morgan had a lot of work to catch up on, of course, so he began to spend night after night working late at the office. I wasn't totally immature. I realized he was president of a major corporation and that he had responsibilities to meet. But I couldn't handle the fact that Morgan expected me to change overnight from an active, thinking woman preparing herself for a career into a doll whose only function was to look decorative."

"You were bored?" Joan asked.

"Bored . . . frustrated . . . lonely. There were servants to do all the housework and cook all the meals. Mr. Kent senior still went to the office every day. Morgan's stepsister was enrolled in a company training program. Sometimes I spent the whole day without speaking to anyone unless I discussed the weather with the cleaning staff."

"Didn't you explain how you felt to Morgan?"

"It was hopeless." Brooke jumped up from the sofa and started to stride agitatedly around the room. "He kept saying, *You're my wife,* as if that meant I automatically had plenty to keep me occupied. We started to argue about everything. He wanted a baby and I refused. It seemed to me that our relationship was too shaky to bring a baby into the picture, but Morgan didn't understand that either. It was awful, Joan. We'd been so happy, and suddenly we couldn't be in the same room without shouting at each other."

Joan sprang up from her chair. "Stay right where you are," she said. "I'll be back in a second." She returned moments later with a bottle of white wine and two glasses. "To hell with the coffee," she said. "This is definitely a session that calls for something a bit stronger! Here, Brooke, take this." She held out a brimming glass of chilled wine.

Brooke accepted it gratefully. "There's not much more to tell," she said between sips. "Morgan's younger brother, Andrew, worked for the family company, too, but he didn't take his work very seriously. In fact, Andrew tried hard not to take life seriously at all. Morgan worked every weekend, but Andrew was always ready to take me sailing or on a picnic or skiing. He often drove with me into Boston so we could see the latest show at an art gallery or tour one of the museums. By the time I realized he was in love with me, it was too late to change the patterns we'd established. Andrew had become dependent on me, just as I was dependent on him. He found it tough to live up to his family's expectations, and I found it impossible to become the sort of mindless wife Morgan seemed to want. Andrew confided in me once that he felt as though he'd lived all his life in his brother's shadow, and naturally he rebelled, just as I did. He went to wild parties, then relied on me to cover up for him when he came home drunk. He used to play hooky from the office, trying to prove to himself that he wasn't totally dominated by his brother and his father."

"You should have insisted on moving into your own apartment, Brooke. No newlyweds can get their marriage on a sound footing when they're living with a bunch of in-laws."

"I did try to suggest that to Morgan," Brooke said.

"But it was like talking to a stone wall." She sighed deeply. "I was naive¹ when we got married, I guess, thinking that life would be all honey and roses because I saw stars every time Morgan took me in his arms. But our problems weren't all my fault."

Joan looked thoughtfully at her empty wine glass, then poured herself another generous helping. "You want some more?" she asked Brooke.

"Why not? Drowning my sorrow in drink is about the only solution I haven't tried."

Joan glanced up from her examination of the wine. "Your marriage had a rough start, I can see that. But nothing you've told me explains why you left your husband and for two years never allowed a single reference to him to cross your lips. I thought . . . we all thought . . . he was dead."

"I don't know if I can talk about it." Brooke's hand was shaking so badly that she was forced to put her wine glass down. She walked across the small living room and stared out the window onto the familiar, dusty courtyard, avoiding her friend's gaze. "Morgan and I . . . we had a terrible row," she said at last. "Two terrible rows, in fact. Andrew came home from a party late one night, and he was almost too drunk to know what he was doing. He came to my room—Morgan wasn't home—and told me he loved me, that Morgan left me alone too much, that I deserved a better husband. All I could think about was taking him back to his own bedroom and getting him into bed. I was afraid he would pass out and hurt himself if he didn't lie down somewhere flat. I was wearing a robe because I'd been reading while I waited for Morgan to come home. You can guess the rest. Morgan came into his brother's bedroom and found me stretched out across Andrew's bed, apparently in a passionate clinch. I was actually unbuttoning Andrew's shirt when Morgan walked in, but he was too furious to stop and discover for himself that Andrew was blind drunk. He almost dragged me from his brother's bedroom. He was very . . . cavemanlike." Brooke's attempt at a smile was hopelessly unsuccessful.

"I see. Isn't it strange that Morgan went to his brother's room? Was he expecting to find you there for some reason?"

"I don't know." Brooke twisted uncomfortably as she told the lie. She had always known why Morgan stormed into his brother's bedroom. Sheila had sent him there. She had spent weeks poisoning Morgan's mind with sly hints as to the relationship between his brother and his wife. Sheila might now be genuinely sorry for the way she had behaved, but she had deliberately caused all the trouble she could when Brooke first arrived at Kent House.

"Was that why you left?" Joan asked. Brooke was quiet for so long that her friend added, "I didn't mean to pry. You don't have to tell me if you don't feel ready to confide in anyone."

Brooke walked back to the table and picked up her wine, swallowing it in one defiant gulp. "No, that wasn't why I left," she said. "Morgan and I managed to stick it out for another couple of months, and then I told him I was pregnant. He . . . he wanted me to have an abortion and I wouldn't agree. So I left."

A loud bellow of rage came from the twins' bedroom, and Joan rose reluctantly to her feet. "Drat! I thought it was too good to be true that the children were all keeping so quiet." She looked shrewdly at Brooke's pale face. "You're lucky the babies woke up when they did, aren't you? Because I think you gave me a somewhat edited version of what happened during your last few weeks with Morgan."

Brooke followed her friend into the twins' bedroom. "I don't know what to do next, Joan," she said. "I loved him so much once and he hurt me so badly. Nothing's changed. I can't risk going back to him, I simply can't!"

Joan quickly separated the squabbling toddlers. "I thought twins were supposed to be perfect playmates for each other," she said ruefully. "How come I've got two who fight? Chrissie, stop sticking your fingers in Jenny's eyes." She turned to Brooke. "Let's take them into the kitchen. I'll pour them some juice while I give you the benefit of my advice. Can you carry Jenny so that we keep them apart?"

Brooke was glad to occupy herself for a few minutes escorting the twins to the kitchen and then settling them into their highchairs. When the girls were busily munching on cookies, Joan turned to face Brooke.

"The past is finished," she said. "Andrew is dead and you have a child. How can you pretend nothing has changed since you left Morgan?"

"I meant *he* hasn't changed. Our relationship...I don't know if I could live with Morgan again."

"Can you honestly say you were happy living without him? If so, how come in nearly two years I never saw you go out on a date unless Joe and I forced you to make up a foursome?"

"I wasn't interested in men," Brooke said defensively. "Morgan had left me quite enough problems without taking on any new ones."

"Morgan certainly left you with something," Joan agreed dryly. "Are you sure it was only problems? Morgan may be a devil to live with, but most women sure would give their right arms to have a crack at the job!"

"I want to go back to him," Brooke admitted, astonished as she heard herself voice the wish. "The good times were...very good."

"I'll bet they were," Joan murmured. "On a scale of one to ten, that man has a sex-appeal rating of at least twenty!"

Brooke's cheeks burned with scarlet fire. "Yes," she said at last. "That's what I keep remembering."

Chapter Nine

MORGAN RETURNED FROM NEW YORK late Friday night. Brooke was curled up on a sofa in the living room, trying to read, when she heard the sounds of his arrival, followed by the exchange of a few inaudible words with Sheila.

Her hands tightened on the cover of her book, then her breath exploded in a tiny sigh of relief when she saw Morgan's tall frame poised at the entrance to the room.

"I saw the light," he said. His voice was husky with fatigue, and his face looked weary in the shadows of the doorway.

"Did you have a good trip?" she asked, simply as an excuse to hold him in conversation for a few minutes. Until she saw him, she hadn't realized how hungry she had been for his company. How had she lived away from him for so long? How had she survived the emptiness of nearly two years without Morgan?

"The trip was okay," he said. He walked from the

darkness of the doorway into the pool of light cast by her reading lamp, and she could see that exhaustion was etched into every muscle of his body.

He slumped into an armchair, not attempting to hide his weariness. "The meetings seemed to go on forever," he said. "I feel as though I've spent years facing a hostile jury, trying to explain over and over again why we have to resist this takeover attempt. I've talked myself hoarse."

"Were you successful?"

"I guess so. We have a thirty-day extension of our credit, which should be enough time, providing no massive blocks of shares come on the market."

He looked exhausted rather than triumphant. "Would you like something to drink?" Brooke asked impulsively. "I could make you some tea or hot chocolate or something."

"No thanks, I'm awash in coffee. Sheila and I have both been pouring the stuff into ourselves in an effort to keep awake." He leaned back in the chair, his eyes closing. "Come and sit over here and tell me what's been going on while I've been away."

The hard lines of his face began to smooth out as he spoke, and it seemed pointless to resist his request. Brooke curled up on the floor, resting her back against his legs. She made no effort to move away when she felt his hands brush lightly across the nape of her neck. He lifted her hair, winding his fingers through the thick strands, and still she made no protest. Tomorrow, she promised herself. Tomorrow she would analyze exactly why she was encouraging this dangerous intimacy. But not tonight.

"This is the first time I've relaxed in three days," Morgan said.

"Have you only been gone three days? It seems much longer." When she realized what she had said, she searched for a way to cover up the truth of her too revealing statement. "Andy has crammed at least a week's worth of mischief into these few days," she said hurriedly. "No wonder it seems a long time!"

"The cat?" Morgan guessed with a trace of laughter in his question.

"The cat," Brooke agreed. "Not to mention several hapless worms and snails that he decided to gather from the garden and present to your father." She smiled reminiscently. "Mr. Kent, you'll be pleased to hear, took it in stride."

"How has my father been?" Morgan asked.

"Doing well, according to Angela. He certainly looks a lot better than he did the day I arrived." She hesitated before adding, "I'm glad you brought us here, Morgan. Andy and his grandfather need each other."

A tiny silence followed, and then Morgan stood up. She watched him walk over to the side table where he had left his briefcase. Quickly he unsnapped the locks and pulled out a thin manila folder. He held it out to her.

"I had this drawn up while I was in New York," he said. "I thought you'd like it right away."

She took the folder with hands that shook slightly, flipping it open to examine the document inside.

"It's the custody agreement," she said at last. "You're renouncing all right to claim custody of Andy."

"The New York lawyer who drew up the contract is from a reputable firm," he said. "I could've waited to ask Barnes to draw it up, but I thought you might prefer it this way."

She looked at Morgan's tightly drawn features and felt her heart do a little flip, leaving a lingering ache. Intuitively she knew that the indifference he displayed was only skin deep, and she wondered why she had never recognized that fact before. What was the point in trying to pretend, she asked herself? Why not admit that she still loved Morgan, since there didn't seem to be any way she could deny the truth of the situation.

"Thank you for drawing up the agreement so quickly," she said finally. The urge to touch him, to force him to abandon that concealing mask, was suddenly overwhelming. She walked across the room to his side and kissed him on the corner of his tightly controlled mouth.

For a moment he held his body stiff, out of reach of the softness of her embrace, then with a harsh sound, deep in his throat, he took her into his arms.

"I want you, Brooke," he said between kisses. "I keep remembering how it used to be when we made love."

The buttons of his suit jacket were pressing into her breasts. She wanted to thrust the barrier of his clothes away. She wanted to feel Morgan's hands ripping open her blouse, reaching inside to soothe the ache of longing in her body. "I remember, too," she said, gasping with pleasure as his kiss literally took her breath away.

"Come upstairs to my bedroom," he said.

She forced herself to ignore the desire uncoiling in the pit of her stomach. She reached up and touched her fingers to his mouth. "We can't make love here, Morgan. This isn't the right time or the right place. There are too many bad memories. . . ."

"We'll sweep them away," he whispered against her mouth.

She shivered with the effort of resistance. It would be so easy to say yes, such heaven to surrender to the power of Morgan's lovemaking. But she knew this house wasn't the right place to try to renew their marriage, and she also knew that nothing less than a renewal of their marriage would satisfy her. "Tomorrow is Saturday," she said. "We could spend all day together, somewhere far away from Kent House."

He pushed her out of his arms with barely restrained violence. "I have to sing for my supper, is that it?" he asked bitterly. "No sex without full payment in advance?

The custody agreement only bought me some smiles and a few kisses, so tell me how much I have to pay in order to get you into my bed?"

The pain of his accusation was like a hard blow to her ribs. "You have to pay with compassion and tolerance and understanding," she said harshly. "And sometimes I'm not sure that you'll ever be able to meet my price."

"Brooke . . ."

"Don't say anything!" She ran out of the room before he could see her tears and locked herself into her bedroom. She tried to ignore the sound of his door slamming loudly in the nighttime silence.

She looked at Andy as she wearily began to undress. He was sleeping as peacefully as ever, but for once the sight of her son brought no solace either to Brooke's pounding heart or to her frustrated body. She crawled into bed and lay awake, staring into the darkness. It seemed a very long and lonely night.

Brooke stood at her bedroom window, staring out across the wide sweep of grass. She glanced at her watch. It was almost nine o'clock. She flipped the button on her radio, and the final chords of a Barbra Streisand song faded as the announcer began to read the news headlines. She didn't really listen to his words because her ears were straining for some sound that would indicate Morgan had left his rooms. So far she had heard nothing, although she had been waiting and listening all morning. Was Morgan planning to come to her today, or had last night ruined the fragile relationship they had begun to build?

She could just see a narrow stretch of the driveway where it curved round to meet the highway. A gray Buick, with three shadowy figures inside, drove sedately toward the road. Brooke waved, although she doubted if anyone inside the car could see her. Andy was going to the zoo with his grandfather and Angela Finks. As the minutes passed, Brooke began to think she would have been wise to go with them. Morgan, she decided sadly, wasn't going to come.

The radio announcer began to read the local weather forecast. He was predicting unseasonal ice storms and cold temperatures. Brooke glanced out the window at the sunshine flooding the yard and managed a smile. She wondered why meteorologists never bothered to lift their heads from their radarscopes before they prepared their forecasts. Couldn't they see the sun?

"Good morning. May I come in?"

Brooke swung around at the sound of Morgan's voice, her pulses racing. After all her waiting and listening, she was still unprepared for his arrival.

"Of course you can come in," she said, switching off the radio. She tried to think of something else to say, but her mind was a hopeless blank.

He came to stand beside her, glancing out the window with her. "You seem lost in thought," he said. "Did I interrupt some important planning?"

"Not at all," she replied a little breathlessly. "Actually, I was just watching the nurse drive Andy and your father to the zoo. They're hoping to make an all-day outing of it, so I guess Angela must think your father's health has improved."

"You didn't want to go with them?" Morgan asked.

"No," she said, aware that her voice still sounded unnaturally breathless. "I decided not to go with them."

"Then if you're free, would you like to have lunch with me? We could drive into Boston, if you like."

It's now or never, Brooke thought. She had spent all night planning this, and she wasn't going to chicken out now. She drew in a deep breath. "Your father tells me you still have the cabin near Ossipee Lake. I wondered if you would have time....I would very much like to drive up there with you."

"It's quite a long drive north for one day," Morgan said noncommittally.

"Yes."

He looked at her searchingly, his own expression impossible to read. "Do you need to change your clothes?" he asked finally.

She ran her hands over her beige twill slacks. "No. I need a thicker sweater, that's all." Her raw silk blouse was casually elegant but not very warm.

"Then let's go," he said. "I'll tell Sheila where we're heading and meet you downstairs."

"All right." She turned away to hide the guilt that stained her cheeks with scarlet. Would he guess what she was hoping to do? That she hoped to keep him at the cabin overnight? "I'll be in the kitchen," she said. "I'm going to beg a few supplies from the cook. It would be...I thought I could cook lunch for us at the cabin since there are no restaurants nearby."

He was silent for a tense second or two. "I have to be in Boston early tomorrow morning, Brooke," he said.

The blush in her cheeks darkened still further. "Of course," she replied with feigned lightness. She took care to keep her face averted. "I think we should try to get back here in time for dinner tonight, don't you?"

"That would certainly be sensible," Morgan said. Since she didn't dare look at him, the thud of her bedroom door as it closed was the only indication that he had left the room.

The atmosphere inside Morgan's Jaguar had been decidedly tense during the ninety-mile drive. It had been her fault, Brooke conceded silently. It was one thing to fantasize about seducing your estranged husband. It was another thing altogether to put such plans into action. She wanted to keep Morgan away from Kent House for the night, but what if the meeting in Boston he had mentioned was an important one?

She shivered slightly as she followed Morgan along the rough stone path to the cabin. It was colder here at the foot of the mountains than it was in Rendford. She watched a flock of wild geese fly over the cabin while Morgan unlocked the rough cedar door.

"Are you coming in?" Morgan asked.

"Oh, yes!" she said hurriedly. "I was just admiring the view. The lake looks fabulous with the sun slanting across it like that. I'd forgotten how beautiful this area is, not to mention how isolated."

Morgan's gaze flicked from the pine-bordered lake and skimmed briefly over her flushed cheeks. "We bought this property so that we could be alone," he said neutrally. "We didn't want neighbors to intrude." He shouldered open the door and carried the small box of supplies into the kitchen. "I've come here quite often in the past two years," he added.

Alone? Brooke wondered. Or with some woman to warm the loneliness of the cool nights—just as she had done during the wonderful early days of their marriage. Morgan had brought her here for their honeymoon, laughing and feathering her cheeks with tiny kisses as he presented the deeds of the cabin to her. "Our very own love nest," he had whispered teasingly. "It's so isolated nobody would believe we're a respectable married couple!"

"I've put the groceries on the counter," Morgan said, interrupting her rush of memories. "I'll go and switch on the generator so that you can start lunch. I'm starving. And I'll start the pump for the well as soon as we have electricity. Let the water run for a couple of minutes before you use it."

She wandered restlessly around the cabin, waiting for the power to come on. The cabin was small but sturdily built of natural wood shingles. The interior was roughly divided into two areas. The kitchen/living/sleeping space all formed a single room, which was dominated by a huge limestone fireplace. The bathroom was conventionally enclosed behind a white-painted door and, in contrast to the deliberate rusticity of the rest of the cabin, it boasted luxuriously sophisticated fittings. The sunken tub was huge, and the walls were entirely covered with an unusual sea-green ceramic tile. The floor tiles gleamed in the same unusual shade, swirled with touches of white and a darker green. Brooke peered uncertainly into the depths of the bathtub. She was relieved to see that no spiders had found their way up the drainpipes since the cabin was last occupied.

She returned to the main room, where Morgan was already occupied in laying a fire. Her breath caught in the back of her throat as she watched him stack kindling beneath the logs. The muscles of his shoulders rippled under the thin fabric of his sweater, and she shivered with reawakened awareness of his potent sexual appeal. He was wearing tight jeans that, according to the label, had been manufactured by a chain discount store. They were now faded by many washings. His cashmere sweater, which had probably cost the equivalent of a week of Brooke's wages at Tony's, hung loosely on his body. Such casual mixing of the highly expensive and the downright cheap was typical of Morgan, she thought. At this moment he looked more than ever like the living, breathing personification of every woman's sexual fantasy, and Brooke wondered bleakly just how many women had felt the potent force of his lovemaking during the last two years.

The flame caught, consuming the dry tinder, and started to lick at the heavy logs. Morgan turned around and gave her an unexpectedly charming grin. "Only one match," he said. "Do I get my boy scout medal?"

"I guess so," she said, unable to resist returning his smile. The leaping firelight seemed to be reflected in his eyes, darkening their usual icy-gray color to a glowing warmth. "It's late, I'll make lunch," she said quickly, not quite ready to admit to herself that she would have been perfectly willing to forgo the meal if only Morgan would take her into his arms. "Soup," she said as she hurried behind the kitchen counter. "I have cream of mushroom soup and French bread. There's cheese, too, and some apples."

His eyes were still laughing at her. "You seem prepared to withstand a siege," he said. "We're only going to be here for a couple of hours, aren't we?"

"Yes, yes, of course," she said, turning on the tiny electric stove. "Is everything still in the same place as it used to be?"

"Here in the cabin," he said, "I don't think anything has changed."

After hearing such words, Brooke thought it was a miracle that she managed to produce the simple meal without any major mishap. Morgan wandered out to the car and returned with a portable cassette player that also contained an AM radio. He ignored the radio and selected a tape, and soon the rich, restrained sounds of an eighteenth-century concerto filled the room.

They sat on comfortable chairs in front of the fire, their lunch spread out on the room's only table, a large, low slab of solid maple. It was incredibly peaceful sitting in front of the crackling logs, listening to the faint stirrings of wind in the pine trees and the occasional call of wild ducks traveling on their journey south.

"In a minute I'll make some coffee," Brooke said. "But right now I'm too lazy to move."

"I'll make it," Morgan said. He came back a few minutes later with two mugs emitting fragrant steam. "Instant," he said. "I'm afraid my energy didn't extend to finding a percolator." He put the cups on the cork mat that protected the smooth maple surface of the coffee table, then sat down on the floor next to Brooke's chair, his long legs stretched out toward the fire. "You're going to have to say something terribly witty and entertaining or I'm going to fall asleep."

Brooke laughed. "Don't you know better than to make a request like that? Ordering me to be entertaining is enough to dry up my thought processes for a week!"

"Then you'll have to think of some other way to keep me awake," Morgan murmured. There was silence in the room except for the occasional hiss of moisture escaping from the burning logs. "No inspirations?" he asked softly.

"I'm not sure." She put her empty coffee mug on the table, then slid off her chair onto the floor. "I'm trying to remember some of the methods I used to keep you awake when we were first married." Her eyes were very wide as she looked at him with a hint of unspoken appeal.

"I think you're getting the right idea," he said huskily. "I hope so, anyway. Kiss me, Brooke."

Slowly, hesitantly, she leaned toward him, closing the gap that separated their bodies. She touched his lips with the tip of her tongue, parting her own lips in an instinctive invitation.

With a harsh sound he lowered his mouth, kissing her with lingering pleasure. He wound his fingers through the long, silky strands of her hair, cradling her body within the firm protection of his arms.

She was frightened by the intensity of her response. She had thought she remembered every detail of their lovemaking, but she had forgotten that once Morgan took her into his arms rational thought became impossible. She had planned to remain in control of everything that happened between them this weekend, but when Morgan kissed her like this, she became mindless, a creature of sensation and feeling.

Morgan finally ended the kiss, drawing away from

her to throw another log on the blazing fire. "It's raining," he said. "Maybe we should start the drive home. I imagine you don't want to find that we're stuck here overnight because of icy roads."

Brooke scarcely bothered to glance out the window. Now that Morgan mentioned it, she realized that the bright sunshine of the morning had entirely vanished, leaving the interior of the cabin shadowed by clouds and a curtain of gray rain.

"Why do you think that?" she asked, hiding her eyes behind the veil of her lashes. "Why are you so certain that I want to go back to Kent House tonight?"

Morgan's face and voice were both expressionless. "Because if we stay here much longer, I'll take you into my bed and make love to you. And nothing you say will stop me. Is that what you want to have happen?"

"Yes, please," she whispered. "Please, Morgan, make love to me now."

He looked at her in silence for a long, tension-filled moment before lifting her into his arms and, without another word, carrying her to the double bed set against the wall. He placed her gently on the down quilt and before she had time to feel chilled, his warm body was lying next to hers.

His hands moved with tantalizing tenderness over her face and shoulders. She trembled with need even though they were both still fully clothed. She felt an answering shudder in Morgan's body, and she reached up to kiss his mouth with an almost convulsive longing. When she thought she wouldn't be able to bear another moment of such glorious torture, being so close to him yet still so far away, he slipped his hands inside her blouse, pushing aside the fragile lace of her bra and cupping her full breasts. His fingers moved to her midriff, tracing a delicate pattern over her rib cage, until his roving hands finally came to rest again on her naked breasts.

His mouth lifted from hers and began a slow journey

along the line of her jaw and down her slender throat. His lips hovered for an instant at the shadowed hollow between her breasts, and then his tongue began to flick fire over her sensitive skin.

Her entire body seemed to ache with unfulfilled passion. "Love me, Morgan," she said as her body arched beneath his touch. "I've been waiting so long."

His soft laugh was triumphant, but when he spoke his voice shook with a need as great as her own. "I'm only too delighted to fulfill your request, my love, but your jeans are more effective than a medieval chastity belt!"

Her fingers were clumsy as they moved to the fastening. As soon as she had undone the stiff metal button, Morgan lifted her hands away, opening the zipper and sliding the tight denim down over her thighs. A knife thrust of delight cut through her as he kissed the smooth skin of her stomach. When he felt her response, his mouth moved away to caress her thighs, and tiny circles of fiery pleasure began to radiate out all over her body.

"Morgan?" she whispered, wanting to ask him if he too felt the exquisite torment of desire that ravaged her senses.

He didn't answer her with words. He stopped her question with another kiss, and his thumb brushed simultaneously across her nipples. Her body shuddered on the edge of ecstasy as she felt the length of his body cover her completely at last.

"I don't think I can wait much longer, Brooke, my love," he groaned against her mouth.

She felt the urgency of his need as an echo of her own desire. "Don't wait," she said. "I want you to love me, Morgan." She lost all awareness of time and place as he took final, triumphant possession of her body.

Afterward, she could only remember that she whispered his name over and over again as the explosion of desire detonated inside her.

It seemed a lifetime before she returned to reality. She

had no idea how much time had passed before she opened her eyes and discovered that she was still lying on top of the down quilt, her legs inextricably intertwined with Morgan's. She shivered as the chill of the air struck her naked body.

He felt her slight tremor. Before she could say anything, he got off the bed and lifted the covers so that she could slip beneath their warmth. Tentatively she touched her fingers to his rough cheek. He turned his mouth and pressed a tiny, hard kiss against her palm.

She was reluctant to break the warm and peaceful silence. The lines of weariness that had scored Morgan's face were gone, leaving him looking both younger and less harassed. His eyes seemed darker than their usual cool gray, but his habitual barriers were back firmly in place, and she found it impossible to interpret the emotions he was screening so carefully.

"Brooke . . ."

"Yes?" She turned in his arms, nestling her head against his chest so that he wouldn't be able to see the mixture of love and longing written so clearly on her face.

"What are you thinking about right now?"

"You," she replied honestly. "Us. And what happens next."

"How about a soak in the tub?" he said with an unexpected trace of laughter in his voice. "Did you notice that I've had a whirlpool attachment installed? I think a man and a woman with creative imaginations could come up with all sorts of exciting ways to use that tub."

She pretended indignation, sitting up in bed and remembering just in time to pull the sheet up with her. "Morgan Kent, I'm shocked," she said. "And just why did you have a whirlpool installed? To entertain your girlfriends?" She was glad that her long hair screened her face, preventing him from seeing how much importance she attached to his reply.

There was a moment's silence. "I've never brought any woman here but you," he said at last.

"Two years of celibacy, Morgan?" she asked with false lightness. "Do you expect me to believe that?"

He avoided her eyes, but she could see the wash of color that stained his cheeks. "Couldn't you tell?" he asked gruffly. "My God, I thought it was all too obvious that I was starving for you."

She was shaken by the raw need still darkening his voice, and her body trembled with an immediate, uncontrollable response to the sensual invitation of his words. "I think maybe we should take that bath," she said huskily. "My creative imagination is beginning to work at full power."

She was in his arms almost before she had finished speaking. He crossed the living room, which was almost dark, now that the fire was dying, and thrust open the bathroom door, managing to keep one arm around her as he turned on the faucets. The hot water poured into the tub, and when he switched on the whirlpool, bubbles frothed high up the sides.

He stepped into the foaming water, tugging Brooke's arm to make sure that she followed suit. She gave a faint gasp as the water swirled round her, binding her body to Morgan's in soft, warm circles of foam.

"I don't believe we ever made love in a bathtub," Morgan said as his hands roamed erotically over the smooth skin of her back. "That was a careless omission on our part, don't you think?"

"I'd prefer to call it life preserving." Brooke gasped as his mouth wreaked havoc with her senses. "Morgan, I'm afraid I may drown if you don't stop. . . ."

"But what a heavenly way to go," he murmured. He gave a sudden groan, all laughter fading from his face. "Hold me, Brooke," he said unevenly. "Touch me . . . feel how much I want you. . . ."

His lips roamed over her skin, tasting the wetness,

and he pulled her urgently against his body. She closed her eyes, dizzy with the pleasure of his touch. "Morgan," she whispered. "Oh my God, Morgan...." And once again she fell into the fathomless brightness of ecstasy.

Chapter Ten

MORGAN STACKED BROOKE'S empty plate on top of the small pile of dishes.

"I'll carry these into the kitchen," he said. "If I don't move, I'll start growing roots in front of the fire."

"It's a good place to be rooted," Brooke murmured lazily. She yawned, then stretched luxuriously as she watched Morgan walk into the kitchen.

"That was another terrific meal, Brooke," he said, putting the dishes in the sink.

"I discovered some interesting cans in your cupboard. We could stay here for a week and not be hungry."

He remained silent. "Don't tempt me," Morgan said finally. "I have to be in Boston when the stock market opens on Monday morning. If I can hang on to the outstanding Kent Industries shares for one more week, I think the conglomerate will give up its attempt to take my company over. They've had a much tougher fight on their hands than they ever anticipated."

"I hope you'll be successful, Morgan, I really mean that. I know the company is the most important thing in your life."

"It certainly used to be," he said shortly. He returned to the fire, but instead of sitting down on the rug next to Brooke, he stared out the window into the darkness. "The weather out there looks pretty grim from what I can see of it," he said.

"Is it still raining? It sounds as if it is."

"It's definitely doing something, but it's hard to see what. It looks more like an ice storm than rain. I think we ought to start planning the drive back to Kent House, because I would guess it's going to be a rough journey."

Brooke stood up and joined Morgan at the window. She leaned against him, deliberately pressing her breasts against the solid muscles of his arm. She felt the sudden rigidity of his body and gave a silent, inner sigh of relief because he still wanted her. Perhaps if she could persuade him to spend the night here...If they slept together in the warm intimacy of the double bed, she would be able to convince him to give their marriage another chance. Surely their passionate lovemaking must mean that he still felt something for her. Surely all those tender love words and soft caresses had been more than the outpourings of a temporary moment of desire.

"Do we have to go back to Kent House tonight?" she asked. "It's Sunday tomorrow. We could wait until lunch time, when the temperature is at its highest, and make the drive in less than two hours. You'd still be back at Kent House in plenty of time to get to your office first thing on Monday morning."

"There's no phone in this cabin, Brooke. How would anybody reach us if there's an emergency?"

"What could possibly happen?" she asked, deliberately closing her mind to the dozens of potential crises that might demand their presence. "Nobody will worry about us. Sheila knows where we planned to go, and Angela Finks will look after Andy."

For some reason Morgan chose not to point out the all-too-obvious holes in Brooke's reasoning. "That's a great idea," he said, "as long as the weather doesn't get any worse. Remember, we have nearly twenty miles of country roads to cover before we hit the main highway."

"It's not even November yet," she said. "And it's raining, not snowing. We're not going to get cut off in the cabin."

"Tell me something, Brooke. Why do you want to stay here? For that matter, why did you suggest that we come here in the first place?"

She walked away from him, bending down to place another log on the fire. She was glad that the heat of the blaze disguised the flush of embarrassment in her cheeks. She had no idea how a woman was supposed to tell her estranged husband that she had planned to seduce him, especially when her plan had already met with pretty spectacular success. "It just seemed like a good idea," she mumbled after a long pause.

He evidently wasn't satisfied with her reply. He strode to her side, pulling her to her feet and gently framing her flushed face in his hands. "Let's try being honest with one another for once, Brooke. I'll ask you again. Why did you suggest that we should come here?"

She jerked her head away from his hands. "I wanted to make love to you," she said, angry at being forced to make the admission. "You're a very sexy man, Morgan, or haven't any of your other women bothered to tell you that?"

"And why do you think *I* agreed to come with *you?*" he asked with a touch of irony in his voice. "God knows there are other things I ought to be doing this weekend." When he saw that she wasn't going to answer him, he put his arms around her waist, pulling her back against his body. "I agreed to come to the cabin because I wanted to make love to you," he said, parroting her words. "You're a very sexy woman, or haven't any of your other lovers bothered to tell you that?"

"There haven't been any other lovers, Morgan, not since the first day I met you."

She felt rather than heard the sudden sharp intake of his breath. "Brooke, look at me," he ordered.

She turned around within the circle of his arms, almost frightened by the desperate urgency of his words. Despite his command, she kept her gaze averted, because she was afraid of what she might see if she looked directly into his eyes.

"Don't look away," he said. "Brooke, tell me the truth. I'm just about going crazy with needing to know. Is Andy my son?"

The silence in the cabin seemed to stretch out forever. "Yes," she said at last. "Andy is your son. His full name is Morgan Andrew Kent. I call him Andy in honor of your father, Morgan, not in honor of your brother."

A convulsive shudder racked Morgan's frame. "I think I've known ever since I forced you to run away from Kent House that you were pregnant with my child, not with my brother's," he said. "Once you'd actually gone from our lives, it was as if I could see clearly again after months of blindness. Can you guess what it was like for me, hoping...fearing...that you were pregnant with my child and not knowing where to find you?" He gave a brief, hard laugh that contained no trace of humor. "There's an example of typical male arrogance for you. However bad it was for me, I know it must have been a hundred times worse for you, bringing up a child alone."

"If you thought Andy was your child, why did you act so angry when you finally found me?"

"I wasn't angry," he said. "I was half-crazy with anxiety. I wanted to get you safely back to Kent House before you could run out on me again. My God, Brooke, I couldn't have stood another two years of searching for you and . . . my son."

"Do you still find it hard to say those words, Morgan? Your brother was my friend, but he was never my lover."

"I treated you very badly two years ago," he said. "Do you think you'll learn to forgive me for the way I behaved?" He stared searchingly into her eyes, his body tense as he waited for her answer.

"You hurt me, Morgan," she acknowledged. "But we both made mistakes. . . ."

Before she could say anything more, he bent his head and covered her mouth in a warm, supplicating kiss.

"I don't care how you feel now," he muttered against her lips. "I'll *make* you forgive me."

A sudden crash of thunder startled them, followed almost immediately by a flash of lightning. The interior of the cabin was illuminated by a flare of incandescent light. Morgan lifted his head and gave her a crooked, self-mocking smile that made her heart lurch.

"I'm relieved to discover that the storm is real," he said. "For a moment there I wasn't sure if the thunder and lightning were just part of the special effects. You pack a pretty potent kiss, woman."

"It's all part of the service," she replied, with an airiness that bore no relationship to the way she was really feeling.

Morgan walked to the door of the cabin and pulled it open cautiously. The force of the wind almost tore the door from his grasp. He had to thrust his shoulder against the sturdy wooden panels in order to shut it. Once it was closed, the howling of the wind and the harsh ping of hailstones faded into the background. The warm, firelit room seemed doubly appealing in contrast to the stormy weather outdoors.

"Thank heavens we're inside," Brooke said.

Morgan looked at her wryly. "Things could get worse rather than better," he said. "I think we'd better switch on the radio and see if there are any special storm warnings out for this area. If it snows on top of this hail, the roads might become impassable for days."

"You mean if the weather forecast's bad, we ought to leave tonight? In this storm?"

"I mean that we really ought to have left hours ago," he said grimly.

"I'm glad we didn't," Brooke said softly.

Morgan broke the sudden tension in the room by reaching for the portable stereo he had brought in from the car. It had rested, neglected, on the corner of the coffee table ever since the original tape had played itself out. He pressed a couple of switches and the voice of a radio disc jockey filled the room. Quickly Brooke laid her hand over Morgan's. "Who wants to listen to the radio," she said. "I have a dozen better ideas about how we can spend our time."

Morgan's fingers stilled beneath her touch. "Sometimes I think you must be a witch," he said, his voice thickening with passion. "Why do I keep on wanting you, over and over again?"

Because you love me, she wanted to cry as he pulled her to him in a rough, hungry embrace. Tell me that you love me, Morgan, she pleaded silently. Tell me that you love me as much as you desire my body.

But he said nothing. He lifted his head from their kiss and gave a small, rueful shrug. "One of us has to show some sign of common sense," he said. He reached again for the radio dial. "Let's see if I can find a weather forecast."

Brooke didn't bother to reply. Somehow it had become imperative that she persuade him to spend the night at the cabin. He had already admitted how much he wanted her. With a little more time perhaps he might be persuaded to acknowledge that he still loved her.

She knelt beside him, spreading her fingers wide against his chest and feeling the thud of his heartbeat beneath her hand.

"Who cares about the weather?" she murmured, finding the carved buckle of his belt and beginning to undo it.

"Anybody with a grain of common sense," he replied tersely.

One of her hands now rested inside his jeans and the other stroked the tanned flesh covering his rib cage. "I don't want to have the radio on," she said. "I want to be able to hear you whisper my name when we make love." Slowly, provocatively, she brushed her lips over the pathway just traced by her hands.

Morgan's breath emerged in a harsh moan. "My God, Brooke, what are you doing?"

"Come to bed and I'll tell you," she murmured. "Better yet, I could show you all over again."

Morgan swept her into his arms. "Witch...." he said.

"The radio...." she reminded him.

Impatiently he flipped the switch, cutting off the announcer's voice in mid-sentence. "I'm waiting for my lessons," he said.

The cabin was still dark when Brooke awoke on Sunday morning. The storm seemed to have stopped, but the wind still howled with an eerie ferocity, and the room felt cold because the fire had burned out during the night. She shivered, pleased to curl up against the warmth of Morgan's body.

At the touch of her legs against his thigh, he stirred sleepily, smiling as he turned to greet her. His face was shadowed by the night's growth of beard, but he looked more relaxed and refreshed than Brooke could remember seeing him.

"Hello," he said.

"Hello." She returned his smile, nestling back under the covers with a pleasant feeling of indolence. Morgan stretched once, then sprang out of bed in a single, athletic movement. Brooke watched him and groaned.

"What's the matter?" he asked, looking concerned.

"You always were obnoxiously wide awake first thing in the morning," she complained, laughing. "Can't you take pity on the rest of humankind and turn down those energetic vibrations a bit?"

He grinned. "You have to learn to take the good with the bad, honey." He ran impatient fingers through his tousled thatch of hair, his expression sobering. "I can't afford to spend any more time in bed, Brooke. We have a lot to do this morning if we're going to leave the cabin in good shape before we set off for home." He pulled on a pair of jeans, then walked over to one of the windows and opened the blinds. "My God!" he said. "I can't believe what I'm seeing!"

Brooke felt a quiver of dismay. "What is it?" she asked. "What's the matter?"

"Snow," he said succinctly. "And it looks about five feet deep except for the drifts, which could be ten feet deep. I'm hoping that's an optical illusion.

Brooke hurried out of bed and came to stand beside him. Despite his warning, she gulped in disbelief when she looked out of the window. All she could see was pristine white snow stretching in every direction. If she hadn't known there was a driveway leading around the lake from the county road, she would have thought the cabin had been miraculously built in the middle of virgin forest. The pine trees and the lake provided the only landmarks. Nothing more than a rough hump and a gleam of glass marked the spot where Morgan's Jaguar was buried.

"I'd better check out the depth of the snow," Morgan said grimly.

"And I'll make breakfast while you're gone. Morgan..."

"Yes?"

"What are you going to do if the snow is too thick for us to drive in?"

His mouth tightened ominously. "I don't know," he said. "I'll face that problem when I get to it."

"I'll start making breakfast," she repeated unhappily.

He glanced at his watch. "Lunch would be more like it," he said dryly. "It's almost noon."

Brooke tried to hide her growing feeling of panic. She had assumed it was still early because it was very dark inside the cabin, but now she began to realize that their chances of returning home today were remote. And it was *her* fault that they were stranded in the wilds of New Hampshire. *She* had enticed Morgan to bed and made him stay overnight against his better judgment. She pushed her hair behind her ears in a nervous gesture, turning away from Morgan's scrutiny as she went into the kitchen and began to prepare their meal.

She had finished her preparations by the time he returned. "What's it like outside?" she asked anxiously. She disliked the thought that her obstinacy might cause Morgan real problems. With Kent Industries threatened by a takeover bid, there could hardly be a less appropriate moment for Morgan to be out of touch with his office.

He pulled off his jacket, dropping it over the back of a chair, and she noticed how his cheeks were reddened by the biting cold of the wind. "We're not going to make it home today," he said with a shrug of resignation. "The wind is blowing the loose snow so that in places you can scarcely see two feet in front of your nose. Even if they get road crews out to clear the county highway, it will take me the rest of the afternoon to dig out the driveway and make sure that the car engine is still in good shape. Thank heaven there's a snow blower in the service hut."

Brooke gulped. "Then what are we going to do? How are you going to get to your meetings? There's no phone and the car doesn't have a CB. Were those meetings very important?"

He shrugged again. "Important enough, I guess."

"I'm sorry, Morgan, it's my fault. I shouldn't have asked you to stay last night. We should have left after lunch, as you wanted to do."

His mouth quirked into a faint smile. "I don't think I was as anxious to leave as you seem to imagine. You didn't persuade me totally against my will, you know. After all, I can call a board meeting any time I want, but it isn't every day that I'm reconciled with my favorite wife."

Her heart flipped, and for a moment she forgot the snowstorm. "Is that what we are, Morgan?" she asked. "Reconciled?"

His gray eyes darkened. "I hope so," he said. "I think our marriage deserves another chance. Are you willing to try again, Brooke?"

She came and stood beside him, pushing nervously at the long, loose strands of her hair. "I'd like to," she said. She did her best to sound coolly rational, since Morgan had said nothing at all about loving her or even desiring her. "I've known for a long time that Andy needs his father."

Morgan smiled. "He was more perceptive than either of us. He realized he had to call me *Dadda* right from the first."

"Andy may be the smartest of all of us, but I think we're both wiser people than we were two years ago. I made too many demands on your time, Morgan, and I didn't understand the pressures you often had to work under."

"Is this confession time?" he asked lightly. "The moment when we finally admit all our past errors? If so, why don't we sit down and eat breakfast while we talk? It might make the whole process a bit less painful."

"Sounds like a good idea," Brooke agreed. "You take the coffee percolator to the table, and I'll bring the rest of the food on a tray."

When they had spread out the food and were sipping hot coffee, Morgan leaned back in the armchair. "Okay," he said. "First confession. You used to accuse me often enough of being a closet chauvinist, and I realize now that you were right. During most of our marriage I operated under a subtle double standard."

Brooke smiled. "What makes you think your chauvinism was subtle? I'd have said it was blatant myself!"

"I plead guilty. I admit I made no effort to understand why you wanted to continue with your career. I knew that museum personnel earn relatively low salaries, and since my own income was sufficient to provide us both with a high standard of living, I didn't bother to think beyond the apparent economic facts."

"And now you're totally reformed?"

"Totally," he said with a grin. "I read *Ms.* magazine from cover to cover each month, and I march in all the demonstrations in favor of ERA."

"All of them?" she queried dryly, although her heart felt as though it was melting every time he flashed her one of his devastating smiles.

"Well, several of them," he amended. He caught her frankly disbelieving expression. "Would you believe some?" he said. "Maybe one or two?"

"I'll believe you attended one demonstration," she said teasingly. "Purely as a gesture of good will, you understand."

He smiled, but she saw his expression tighten as he glanced at his watch. "What were your meetings about, Morgan?" she asked. "Why did you need to go to your office on a Sunday?"

"It was connected with the takeover bid. Technical financial matters. I won't bore you with all the details."

She realized then just how often she must have cut off his attempts to talk about his business in the old days of their marriage. "I'd like you to tell me," she said quietly.

He looked at her searchingly for a moment before speaking. "I asked some of the corporate financial staff to meet with my investment bankers from New York," he said finally. "We planned to have an up-to-the-minute assessment of the number of shares outstanding . . . how many I control personally . . . how much cash I have on hand. I thought there was a good chance that we'd be able to make a public statement on Monday saying that the takeover bid has failed."

"And you think that chance will be lost if you don't get back in time for the meetings?"

"No," he said, after a slight pause. "There's no real reason to suppose that my absence for an extra day will make much difference. The announcement will simply be delayed, that's all. I guess I'm worried about my absence because, with a takeover bid, seizing the right moment is all-important, and I think that when the stock market closed on Friday I controlled sufficient shares to reject the takeover offer outright. My bankers and I had a long conversation first thing on Saturday morning. Things were looking pretty good."

Brooke got up from the table and stared apprehensively out the window. It was now well past noon, but not even a gleam of sun penetrated the leaden clouds. The high winds of the previous night had blown away the last few leaves from the trees, and the skeletal outlines of their bare branches, laden with frozen snow, were outlined against a somber background of gray sky.

"Morgan," she said, "what happens if the weather is still just as bad tomorrow?"

"The county roads will be plowed and sanded by tomorrow morning," he said. "And I'm determined to make it out of our lane even if I have to push the Jaguar down the entire length of the driveway."

"I'm sorry about the delay, Morgan, I really am. This is going to seem a wasted day for you."

She saw his teeth flash in a sudden, wolfish smile. "I wouldn't say that exactly." His hands came around her waist, pulling her back against his body. "I know exactly how I'm going to spend the time, and I promise you it won't be wasted." He turned her around and kissed her passionately so that she had no possible way of mistaking his intentions.

She pretended an outrage she was far from feeling. "What typically male arrogance," she said when she finally recovered her breath. "Don't I get any say in the matter?"

"Sure," he said. "I'm reformed. I'm all for equal rights, remember? I've chosen the activity, so that means *you* get to choose the place." He dropped a deliberately patronizing kiss somewhere in the region of her nose. "Make your big choice, honey. Don't blow this unique opportunity to share in the decision-making process. Do you want us to make love in bed or in the whirlpool?"

"I should prefer to make love in front of the fire," she said with deliberate perversity, adding with heavy sarcasm, "that is, when you manage to get around to lighting it. Or have you reverted to the old caveman idea that tending a fire is woman's work?"

Morgan's smile was teasing as well as triumphant. "You see?" he said, ignoring the last half of her remark. "You've just admitted you want to spend the day making love to me. Since I'm a reasonable man, there's no problem about where. We can make love first in front of the fire and then in bed and then in the whirlpool. . . ."

Brooke sighed as Morgan gathered her into his arms.

"Is this how you defeat your business opponents?" she said. "With trickery and wicked deception?"

"No," he said. "But then I've never tried to talk my business opponents into my bed."

Brooke knew there was some appropriately scathing answer to his outrageous remark lurking right on the tip of her tongue. She tossed back her head and found herself staring into Morgan's warm, *loving*, eyes. Her lips parted in a tiny gasp of astonishment, and he kissed her with a promise of such tender passion that she was sure her bones were melting.

"Come to bed," he said enticingly, his voice deep with passion.

For the life of her she couldn't remember the protest she had planned to make. "Oh, yes," she whispered. "Yes, Morgan, please."

They had heard the bulldozers plowing out the county highway around three o'clock in the morning, the noise of the heavy machinery echoing loudly in the stillness of the snow-covered night. Fortunately the wind had dropped some time on Sunday afternoon, so their exhausting efforts in clearing the private lane leading to the main road had not been wasted. Brooke had always prided herself on being physically fit, but an afternoon spent shoveling snow and guiding the snow blower soon corrected that impression. "This machine bucks like a bronco," she yelled at Morgan as she wrestled unsuccessfully with the recalcitrant snow blower.

"You guide it like this," he said, taking over the controls and cutting a swath of snow with infuriating ease.

She muttered something distinctly unladylike under her breath. He grinned and dropped a quick kiss on the nape of her neck. "I'll pretend I didn't hear that remark if you'll go inside and make some hot chocolate. That's the proper place for a wife, isn't it? In the kitchen?"

She didn't consider him adequately punished until she had shoved several handfuls of wet snow deep inside the collar of his sweater. "All right," he said finally, laughing in mock surrender. "A kitchen isn't the proper place for a man to keep his wife." He waited until Brooke was a safe distance away, then shouted, "It's better to keep her in bed!"

Her shoulder muscles were still painful when they got up in the half-light of early Monday morning and prepared to leave the cabin. The faint ache in her body seemed to match the uncertainty in her heart. Was one almost perfect weekend sufficient to wipe out two years of bitter memories? Did she and Morgan have an adequate foundation on which to build a new relationship? She had no doubt that Morgan desired her, and she suspected that he was looking forward to becoming a proper father to Andy. Was that going to prove a sufficient basis for renewing their marriage?

Although she knew it was irrational, she kept hoping that Morgan would sweep her into his arms and proclaim his undying love for her. Naturally, he did nothing so dramatic. In fact, he seemed preoccupied, scarcely glancing at her as they completed the routine tasks that were necessary if they were to leave the cabin clean and weatherproof.

The drive home was a nightmare journey of drifting snow and icy roads. Brooke spent a fair part of the time with her eyes closed, so that she wouldn't have to see the dangerous conditions Morgan was driving through. She was numb with a mixture of fatigue and relief when he finally turned into the driveway of Kent House. She didn't even want to guess at how tired he must be feeling. Fortunately the roads near Rendford were freer of snow and easier to drive on than the narrow highways in the foothills surrounding the cabin. But even here, almost ninety miles south of the cabin, the storm had obviously hit hard. It was difficult to believe that only two days had passed since she and Morgan had driven out of the sun-dappled driveway of Kent House, admiring the brilliant remnants of autumn color as they went.

Andy greeted Brooke with kisses and hugs and little cries of welcome. "Momma," he beamed as soon as he saw her. "Momma come back. Momma kiss. Dadda kiss." He suited his actions to the words, clutching both their hands and chattering happily as he walked between them into the living room. "Here is Gwampa," he said and his face split into a huge, self-satisfied smile. "Gwampa," he repeated. "Gwampa."

Brooke hugged him close, her eyes misty with tears. "Clever boy, Andy," she said. "That sure is a difficult new word you've learned." She smiled shyly at Mr. Kent. "I hope he hasn't been causing you and Angela a lot of trouble."

"Far from it," Mr. Kent said. "Angela, who insists on hovering in the corner there to keep an eye on me, will tell you my health is better than it has been in weeks." He smiled at the nurse as he spoke, then his expression sobered as he reached out to ruffle Andy's hair. "There's nothing like having a toddler around the house for helping an old man put his problems in perspective. But that's enough about us. What happened to you two? Was the storm very bad up at Ossipee?"

"It certainly was," Morgan said. "And completely unexpected. We had no idea it was coming."

Mr. Kent looked surprised. "Didn't you hear any weather reports before you left? The weathermen were predicting this storm ever since Friday night, and for once their forecasts hit it right on the button. From what they said, we knew that the cabin was located just about at the storm center. I was surprised when Sheila told me you'd risked driving up there, but I'm even more surprised that you made it back today. I thought it might be as much as a week before the road crews got around to clearing those country roads of snow. I've been trying to warn Andy that it would be a while before his Momma and Dadda got back."

"Maybe the highway commissioner is running for re-election," Morgan said lightly. "The road was cleared less than eighteen hours after the snow stopped, but even after the plows had gone through it was still quite a drive home. I'm going to shave and take a shower and go to the office," he added. "I expect there have been quite a few calls for me, haven't there? Where's Sheila, by the way? Is she holding the fort at the meetings I arranged?"

"She's gone to New York," Mr. Kent said. "She left on Saturday night before the storm closed down the airport."

"Good. I expect she's trying to explain to the bankers why I disappeared," Morgan said. "Are the messages from the office on my desk?"

"The whole pile," Angela agreed, smiling. "I think every executive in your company must want to talk to you, Morgan. If you come with me, I'll show you where I stacked all the scraps of paper."

"And I'll bring Andy upstairs with me while I take a shower," Brooke said. "I've been wearing the same clothes for three days now, and I'm beginning to feel more than a bit crumpled." She smiled at her father-in-law, then scooped Andy up into her arms. "Want to build a snowman this afternoon?" she asked him as she followed Morgan and Angela out of the room. "Would you like that?"

Angela's relaxed expression altered as soon as the living room door closed behind them. "Morgan, I think you should know that it's been an absolute zoo here this morning. Your office has been calling every fifteen minutes for the last two hours. They're frantic to get in touch

with you. Apparently your brokers have heard rumors
that a huge block of Kent Industries shares were offered
to the conglomerate over the weekend in a private deal,
and your brokers didn't have either the funds or the
authority to make a higher offer without you being here.
I didn't want to worry your father with the news, that's
why I didn't mention anything while we were in the
living room."

Brooke looked quickly at Morgan, and her heart sank
as she registered the unrelieved grimness of his expression. This was precisely the sort of move he must have
been fearing while they were stuck at the cabin.

"I'll leave you to make your business calls, Morgan,"
she said. She tried to find some way of showing her
concern for his problems, but it was difficult to talk
personally when the nurse was within earshot. "I'll be
looking forward to seeing you as soon as you get home
from the office."

"Okay." His response was abstracted and his expression remained forbidding. "Bye, Andy," he said. He
leaned over to give the child a quick hug, and it seemed
to Brooke that he deliberately avoided touching her. He
shot one strangely calculating look in her direction before
turning swiftly away. "We'll talk later," he said. With
a few swift strides he had covered the length of the hall
and turned the corner, out of her sight.

Chapter Eleven

THE DAY SEEMED ENDLESS, and even Andy's obvious delight in having Brooke home again couldn't compensate for the lonely hours without Morgan. When Andy was in his crib for the night, she "read" a picture book to him. He looked admiringly at the drawings of fat cows and yellow ducklings and sniffed the pages, obviously liking their new smell. "Nice," he said several times, running his fingers over the shiny brightness of the colored pages. He fell asleep with the book tucked up inside his security blanket and his teddy bear resting across one ear.

The dinner hour came and went with nothing more than a brief telephone call from Morgan's secretary to inform them that he wouldn't be home until later. Brooke tried to conquer the irrational fear building up inside her. Of course Morgan had a lot to do. Of course he would need to stay later at the office after missing several important meetings over the weekend. But the fear refused to go away. Something was wrong, she thought, and her relationship with Morgan was not nearly strong enough to bear the burden of any misunderstandings.

She played a game of backgammon with Mr. Kent, managing to concentrate just sufficiently to move her pieces in the correct order. She wasn't sorry when he pleaded tiredness and refused her offer of a second match, although that left her with nothing to do except sit in the living room and worry.

At eleven o'clock she went upstairs. She checked Andy, who was sleeping peacefully, then started to pace the floor of her room. After thirty minutes of useless pacing, she quietly let herself out of her bedroom and walked down the corridor to Morgan's apartment. She tested the doorknob. It turned and she slipped inside.

The room was empty, of course. She sat down on one of the armchairs close to the fireplace, wishing a fire was burning in the grate. She kicked off her shoes and curled her legs up under her, staring at the birch logs stacked and ready to be lit. She had no awareness of drifting off to sleep. One moment she was waiting, every nerve strained, for sounds of Morgan's return. The next moment she realized somebody was shaking her, then hauling her to her feet with barely suppressed violence.

She opened her eyes.

"What are you doing here?" Morgan asked furiously. "Are you hoping to seduce me into another forty-eight hours of mindless sex? Surely that's a bit optimistic, even though I've gone a fair way toward proving myself a fool."

She rubbed her eyes, shaking away the clinging mists of sleep. "Morgan...?" she said with evident bewilderment.

His mouth twisted into a harsh sneer. "Cut the innocent act, Brooke. What are you trying to do? Buy a little time while you put some fresh scheme into action?

It's a bit late to start making plans, isn't it? You've had the whole day to think up a convincing story and, God knows, your ingenuity seems to be endless."

"What are you talking about, Morgan?"

"I think that ought to be my line, honey," he said with bitter mockery. "What were you trying to do, Brooke? Exact some sort of revenge for the way I treated you when you were pregnant with Andy?"

She drew in a deep breath in an effort to steady herself. "Would you mind if we started this conversation at the beginning? What exactly am I supposed to have done?"

He thrust her away as if he could no longer bear to touch her. "The shares, Brooke. I'm talking about the shares you owned in *my* company. It wasn't enough for you to sell them, was it? You had to make sure you sold them at the time and in the way that would cause me the most trouble. You wanted me to lose control of Kent Industries—permanently and irretrievably."

"I haven't sold any shares," she said. "What are you talking about, Morgan?"

"For God's sake, Brooke, don't try to pretend ignorance with me. Why lie about things now? Are you waiting for me to congratulate you on your brilliant performance over the weekend? Well, congratulations! Did it give you a kick to see me responding to your wonderful acting? You knew on Saturday morning that this whole area was due for a severe storm. You were listening to the weather report on the radio when I came into your bedroom, and suddenly—after two years of avoiding me—you couldn't wait to suggest that we spend a cozy weekend alone together, miles from civilization. Man, was I a fool!"

"Are you suggesting that I had some special reason for asking you to go to the cabin? Do you think I deliberately kept you away from your office?"

"Didn't you?" he asked bitterly.

"Not exactly."

He laughed disbelievingly. "I admit you did a fabulous job of setting me up," he said. "All those soft caresses and burning kisses that never quite led to fulfillment .... You know exactly how to promise a man paradise while you wait for him to deliver the goods, don't you, Brooke?"

"What goods do you think I was waiting for you to provide?"

"The custody document," he said impatiently. "I sealed my own fate when I handed that over to you, didn't I, Brooke? As long as there was a chance that I might claim Andy, you wouldn't have done anything."

She refused to dignify his accusations with an answer, and he strode over to her side, jerking her head around so that his mouth hovered only inches away from hers. "Such a delectable mouth," he murmured. "And it lies so beautifully. Haven't you got anything to say in your own defense, my sweet, lying wife?"

She tore herself from his grasp, pushing his hands away. "I'm going to bed," she said. "In my own room."

He moved swiftly to pull her back from the door. "I haven't finished with you yet. Don't you want to hear how near your schemes came to success? I'll even admit how willing I was to be persuaded to forget all about my obligations to the company and the people who work for me. Tell me, was it a dreadful bore having to exploit the charms of your body while you waited for the snow to isolate us in the cabin?"

"No." Her throat was so dry that she was amazed she managed to produce even a single intelligible syllable.

Morgan's harsh laughter grated in her ears. "Do you want to hear something funny? I thought maybe you still loved me, despite everything that had happened between us. I thought no woman could make love as sweetly as you did unless she cared. And all the time you were using your body as a trap, a weapon to defeat me."

"Would it be any use if I told you I still don't understand what you're talking about? I think you're saying that somebody sold some shares while we were snowbound in Ossipee. Have you lost control of Kent Industries, Morgan? Is that why you're so angry?"

"Damn it, Brooke, this conversation is becoming absolutely ridiculous. It's well after midnight and I'm too tired to waste time playing perverted verbal games with you. Eight percent of the voting shares of Kent Industries were offered to the conglomerate over the weekend. Eight percent is precisely the amount of stock you own. Moreover, you're the only person with a motive for selling."

"A motive?" A gasp of laughter was torn from her throat, but it sounded more like a sob than an expression of amusement. "And what is my motive supposed to be, Morgan?"

"Revenge," he said. "Retribution for the way I treated you when we were married."

"I see," she said with another tiny, hysterical gasp. "I didn't know you suffered from such a guilty conscience, Morgan." She moved closer to the fireplace, leaning against the rough stones as if to draw support from their solidity. "Tell me, was I successful in this clever scheme of mine? Have you lost control of the company?"

"No, I'm afraid you miscalculated, honey." The anger in his voice twisted the knife deeper into her wounded feelings. "The roads got plowed out quicker than you expected, I guess, and so I got back to Boston just in time to put in a bid on those shares. I had to mortgage everything I possess, including this house, but I came up with the necessary cash. Hasn't your broker called you with the good news? You're a wealthy woman, my dear. Your stock sold this afternoon at four dollars over

Friday night's final trading price."

"Since you managed to buy up the shares, does that mean you're still president and chief executive officer of Kent Industries?"

"I'm sorry to disappoint you," he said sarcastically, "but the answer is yes. I'm sure you'll be devastated to hear that I'm still in complete control. In fact, the management of the conglomerate is conferring with its Japanese directors, and I have high hopes that the chairman will soon announce that he is abandoning his efforts to take over Kent Industries. The conglomerate never anticipated having to put up such a strong fight."

"I'm very happy for you," she said quietly. She looked up, her expression pleading. "You're making a mistake, Morgan. I didn't sell any shares. I wish you'd believe me."

There was a total silence in the bedroom and it seemed to last forever.

"Prove it," Morgan said finally.

Brooke moved away from the fireplace, pacing the room in a vain effort to dissipate some of the tension stretching between them. She clenched her hands so tightly together that she could feel the nails digging little grooves in her palms. She saw the suspicion etched into Morgan's face, and she dropped her gaze to the floor, thrusting her hands into the pockets of her jeans in an unconscious gesture of rejection.

"No," she said with a touch of defiance. "I won't try to prove anything to you, Morgan. If we're going to give our marriage another chance, you have to learn to trust me."

"I'm not asking you to do anything very dramatic," Morgan said. "All you have to do is call the lawyer and give him permission to tell me that he's still acting as trustee for your shares in Kent Industries."

"It's one o'clock in the morning," Brooke pointed

out. "We can't start telephoning people at this time of night. I'm asking you to accept my word, Morgan. Surely that isn't too much for a wife to expect from her husband."

"But we've never behaved like a normal husband and wife, have we? And this doesn't seem an appropriate moment to start." He turned away, raking his hands through his thick hair. "Oh hell! I'm tired and it's too late to try to talk. Can't you understand my problem, Brooke? There's nobody else who *could* have sold those shares, because nobody outside the family owns that many."

"Morgan, if you can't trust my word about something as important as this, then there's no point in pretending we're giving our marriage a second chance. If we can't trust each other, we'll be living a lie." She walked toward the door, so anxious to avoid his accusing eyes that she was scarcely aware of what she was doing. If she didn't leave his room now, before he said something even more hurtful, she wasn't sure if she could be responsible for her actions.

"Where are you going?" he asked.

"At this precise moment I'm going to bed," she said flatly. "Tomorrow I guess I ought to make arrangements to leave Kent House. It would be better if—"

"Like hell it would be better!" he interrupted. "If you think you're going to walk out of here with *my* son, you'd better think again.

He had hurt her so badly by his lack of trust that she responded almost without thinking, her only purpose to hurt him as he had hurt her. "What makes you so sure he is *your son?*" she asked furiously. "You don't believe anything else I say, so why believe that?"

His face turned deathly pale, whether from rage or shock Brooke couldn't tell. "Andy is my son and we both know it," he said harshly. "But just so you don't decide to pack your bags and run off into the night like you did before, I'm going to make damn sure that you have a good reason for staying here."

"There's no good reason for me to stay with you."

"I'll find one," he said. "It's not difficult for me to think of reasons to keep you near me. How about if I make you pregnant again? And this time we'll both be sure—right from the start—that you're pregnant with my child."

"You're crazy if you think I would agree to have another child," she said fiercely. "What makes you think—"

Her words were cut off as he pulled her into his arms and carried her across to the bed, pressing her deep into the pillows.

"I assume this is where you hoped to spend the night," he said tersely. "Otherwise you wouldn't have been waiting for me with such touching, wifely devotion."

"I was waiting for my *husband,* a man who trusts me. You're not that man, Morgan, and I'm beginning to think you never will be."

"You talk too much," he said. "And you don't mean most of what you say."

"You arrogant, chauvinist devil!" she exclaimed. "Of course I mean what I say!"

He ignored her furious words. "At least if I keep you in my bed I'll know you're not trying to run away," he said angrily.

"I don't want to be in your bed," she hissed. "Not now . . . not ever."

"Don't lie," he said, and his mouth moved aggressively to cover her lips, giving her no chance to escape the invasion of his tongue. He stilled the half-hearted protests of her body with his legs, forcing her hands above her head while his hungry gaze roamed over the heaving outline of her breasts. "I want to make love to you," he said. "Whatever we say to each other never seems to destroy the physical attraction between us. That's always been there, and I think it always will be."

"I hate you when you talk like this, Morgan, do you understand? You don't want to make love to me. You just want sex, and I'm not prepared to agree."

"It's too late for you to say that," Morgan said. "It's too late for both of us."

"Will you let me go?" she demanded through clenched teeth, twisting her head in a frantic effort to avoid the tantalizing touch of his lips. "I've told you I want to leave, and I'm not going to change my mind. Do you thing rape is going to solve *anything?*"

"Rape wouldn't solve anything. But this isn't going to be rape."

"Why you arrogant, egotistical..."

"I shouldn't say anything more, Brooke. You're beginning to repeat yourself." She thought she saw the faint hint of a smile before his mouth came down forcefully on hers, shutting off the rest of her words. The tip of his tongue flicked across her lips, but she kept them tightly closed, determined to resist his passion.

"Let me go!" she repeated.

"One kiss," he said thickly. "One kiss and then I promise you can leave."

She opened her mouth to refuse him, but he pressed his lips savagely against hers, demanding submission. She tried to push him away, but when she felt the hard hungry caress of his tongue, her resistance weakened, and she opened her mouth to return his kiss.

He gave a low murmur of triumph when he felt the involuntary sigh that parted her lips and softened her body against his thighs. His own anger seemed to vanish, to be replaced by a tender, coaxing passion. His fingers traced a slow path over her body, weaving chaotic spells wherever they passed. His mouth blazed a trail of erotic fire. All too soon her feeble pretense of indifference gave way to a smoldering, aching need.

When he knew that her resistance was utterly vanquished, Morgan got up from the bed and quickly removed his clothes. As soon as he returned to the bed, he bent his head to kiss the sensitive skin between her breasts. His fingers shook slightly as he fumbled with the clasp of her bra, making Brooke aware of the fact that she exercised as much power over him as he did over her. "Help me take this off," he whispered. "My God, Brooke, I want you so badly."

She didn't say anything, because she didn't want to admit the extent of her own need. She could feel the sheen of sweat that covered Morgan's shoulders, but her own body was so hot with passion that she could scarcely tell where her heat began and Morgan's ended.

"Look at me, Brooke," he said, "and answer me truthfully. If I take you now, is it going to be rape?" His voice was husky as he asked the question, and his mouth rested only a breath away from her own.

She closed her eyes. "No," she said.

"Don't close your eyes, Brooke," he urged. "Look at me and tell me what you want."

Reluctantly she stared into the turbulent gray depths of his eyes.

"I want you," she said, helpless to deny the fierce reality of her feelings. "I need you to make love to me."

She heard the sharp intake of his breath, and recognized his triumph, although she no longer cared that she had given him the victory he sought.

"I need you, too," he admitted as he buried his face in the silken smoothness of her neck. "Hold me," he said. "Tell me again that you want me."

She clung to him willingly as he guided her to the climax of their passion, blind and deaf to everything except the tightly woven world of their mutual need.

Later, much later, as she fell into the deep sleep of exhaustion, she wondered if she had really heard Morgan whisper, *I love you, Brooke*.

At first the persistent ringing of the telephone seemed to be part of her dream, but when she forced herself to full consciousness, she heard the low murmur of Morgan's voice talking softly into the bedside phone. She turned on her side so that she could watch him, and her body ached with unexpressed love as she remembered the tenderness of their previous night's passion.

Deliberately she pushed aside the enticing memories. It was morning now, and in the clear light of day she forced herself to face up to several truths that had been too painful to consider the night before. Brooke knew that she was deeply in love with Morgan, that she wanted their marriage to have a second chance. But she also knew that their relationship couldn't survive without mutual trust. Unless Morgan was prepared to accept her as the person she really was, for both their sakes she had to end the marriage. Not by running away, as she had done before, but legally, by divorce. A physical attraction as intense as theirs, without true love to support it, would ultimately destroy both of them.

Morgan finished his telephone conversation and immediately got out of bed. He didn't look at her until he had thrust his arms into a robe and tightened the belt around his waist.

"That call was from my company's bankers in New York," he said. "They're going to issue a statement today that Kent Industries has successfully fought off the takeover bid. I have to leave for the office right away."

"Then it's all over?" she asked. "After today's announcement there'll be no more chance of you losing control?"

"It will all be over," he agreed. "The takeover bid has

failed." He walked over to the window, avoiding Brooke's eyes. "I might be home late," he said. "Will you be here when I get back?"

"Do you want me to be here?"

"Yes," he said. The phone rang again before he could say anything more. "Damn!" Morgan muttered as he snatched the phone from its cradle. "I wouldn't answer it except that it's on my private business line."

He spoke tersely for several minutes, his brows drawn together in intense concentration. "I have to go," he repeated as soon as he had hung up. "I have to talk to the Japanese owners of the conglomerate. We have to make sure that we come to an amicable arrangement with them now that their takeover bid has failed. We can't afford to have them dumping their holding of shares onto the market all at once. It would depress the share price too much and leave us vulnerable to another takeover attempt."

"Another one?" she said. "You mean you and Kent Industries may have to go through all this *again?*"

His mouth tightened. "It's a possibility," he said. "You already know that running a company like Kent Industries is a demanding job, Brooke, and there would be no point in my pretending that because this takeover attempt has failed, from now on I shall be able to spend most of my summers sailing and my winters skiing." He thrust his hand angrily through his hair. "Oh, what the hell!" he said. "I have to take a shower and get to the office."

She watched him as he walked toward the bathroom, and her stomach churned with nervous uncertainty. At the bathroom door he paused and glanced back over his shoulder.

"Will you wait for me tonight?" he asked. The husky note of appeal in his voice belied the icy calm of his features. "Please, Brooke, don't leave me until we've had a chance to talk."

Her fingers traced one of the geometric designs on the sheet. "I'll wait for you," she said, and then immediately wondered if she had been wise to make such a promise. After all, Morgan hadn't apologized for his accusations of the previous night, and while she could easily prove to him that she hadn't sold any of her shares, she wasn't at all sure that she wanted to spend the rest of her life constantly proving and reproving her innocence.

Andy was crying lustily in his crib when she returned to her bedroom, but his tears of fright quickly turned into a bellow of rage when he saw his mother. He wasn't accustomed to waking up and finding himself alone, and Brooke murmured a prayer of thanks that he hadn't decided to climb out of his crib and start exploring. She washed and dressed him quickly, kissing his nose when it popped through the collar of his chunky-knit blue sweater. She sat him down in the middle of a pile of toys and, after making sure that her bedroom door was closed so that he couldn't wander away, went into the bathroom to take a hurried shower.

She was thinking deeply while she dressed. Last night she had been bitterly hurt by Morgan's suspicions, but this morning she was calm enough to appreciate his dilemma. She pinned her hair into a neat coil on top of her head, trying to see events from Morgan's point of view. He believed that she had lured him up to the cabin and kept him there while her brokers negotiated the sale of her shares. As it happened, he had completely misunderstood her motives, but it was an unlucky coincidence—to say the least—that somebody had sold off a large block of shares at the precise moment she had deliberately set out to seduce Morgan.

She finished dressing and carried Andy downstairs to the kitchen, ready to prepare their breakfast. The heart of the dilemma, she thought, was that *somebody* had sold those shares. Who?

She wrinkled her brows in concentration as she handed Andy his bowl of cereal. She tried to recall her conversations with Mr. Barnes, the lawyer. He had explained exactly how the Kent Industries shares were distributed. Under the terms of Andrew's will, she owned eight percent of the total. Did anyone else own that much? Morgan, of course, but not Mr. Kent senior, who had gradually been selling his shares. How about Sheila?

Brooke expelled her breath in a sudden exclamation. *Sheila* had inherited eight percent of the shares from her mother. Could she have sold her inheritance, knowing what a devastating effect it would have on Morgan? Would she have any compelling reason to do so?

Brooke tried to consider the problem objectively, but her feelings about her stepsister-in-law were too confused for her to assess the situation impartially. She lifted Andy out of his chair, scarcely noticing that her breakfast coffee and toast remained untouched on the table. "We're going to see your grandfather," she said. "Are you ready to go?"

Andy nodded, wriggling with delight. "Gwampa," he said. As soon as his feet touched the floor, he darted out of Brooke's grasp. With the agility of a small monkey he made a lunging dive under the table and emerged holding the cat. "Josh," he announced to his mother, reminding her of the cat's name. "Take Josh to see Gwampa."

"I hope your grandfather is ready for this," Brooke muttered. "I'll hold the cat, Andy. You might hurt his tummy if you try to carry him upstairs."

They found Mr. Kent in his sitting room, chatting to his nurse. He greeted them both with enthusiasm. "Good morning, Brooke. Hi, Andy! How kind of you to bring the cat to see me." Mr. Kent cast a grin in Brooke's direction as he spoke to Andy. "Do you want me to hold Joshua on my lap and stroke him?"

Andy nodded. Like most children approaching two years of age, he could say *no* clearly and distinctly, but he hadn't yet learned to say *yes*. He watched with silent approval as the cat settled down on Mr. Kent's lap, then he stared appealingly into his grandfather's eyes. "Tic-toc?" he asked. When nothing happened, he repeated more firmly, "Tic-toc. *Tic-toc!*"

"Say please," said Mr. Kent as he pulled out his large, old-fashioned watch. He flipped open the case and allowed Andy to stare at the slowly moving gear wheels. "I don't know what the next generation of grandfathers will do," he said with a laugh. "I don't think digital watches are going to have much appeal for two-year-olds."

"Grandfathers are a canny breed when it comes to entertaining their grandchildren, so I'm sure they'll think of something. Don't you agree, Angela?" Brooke smiled at the nurse, glad she was in the room, since her presence would prevent a great deal of awkward explanation. "Mr. Kent," she said, getting to the purpose of her visit, "I'm hoping you can help me. I need to get in touch with Sheila, and I thought you might have a phone number where I can reach her."

Mr. Kent looked up, faintly startled. "There's nothing wrong, I hope?"

"No," Brooke said. "That is, nothing important."

"Andy and I will go and play for a while," Angela said, tactfully retreating to the far corner of the room. "There are a few toys in a box left from Andy's last visit."

"Thanks, Angela." Mr. Kent turned back to Brooke. "I'm happy to give you any information I can. I already mentioned, I think, that Sheila went to New York on Saturday night to be with her fiancé. She had company business to take care of today, so she told me, and the weather looked so bad that she decided to fly out before the authorities closed down the airport."

"I see. I do need to talk with her, although it's probably not important. Do you have her fiancé's telephone number?"

Mr. Kent gave a small smile. "There's no need for you to be so discreet, my dear. I think at the moment I'm more likely to die of curiosity than to break down from worry! Don't you know that unsatisfied curiosity is very bad for my blood pressure?"

Brooke gave him a faint grin. "You're an old phony. You don't have blood pressure problems."

"Well, I'm sure thwarted curiosity must be bad for the general state of my health. Everything else enjoyable certainly seems to be!"

"Could you just take my word for the fact that I really need to ask Sheila a few questions? Right away. . . ."

Mr. Kent's expression immediately sobered. "Of course. Sheila's fiancé lives in Manhattan, and she may still be at his apartment. Or else you could try Morgan's investment brokers. Sheila mentioned she had to see them some time today."

"I'd like both those phone numbers, please," Brooke said. She swung around jerkily when her father-in-law started to get up. "Perhaps I'm leaping to crazy conclusions, Mr. Kent, but can you think of any reason Sheila might have to sell her shares in Kent Industries?"

Mr. Kent's face paled. "Is that what Sheila's done?" he asked hoarsely. "Sold her shares? Has Morgan lost control of the company?"

"Oh, no! The company's quite safe," Brooke said hastily. "Everything at the office is fine, I promise you. When Morgan left this morning, he seemed confident that the takeover bid was going to fail."

She was relieved to see how quickly Mr. Kent recovered his composure once she had reassured him about Kent Industries. "I'm all right," he said, waving away her offer of a glass of water. "But you haven't answered my question. Has Sheila sold her shares?"

Brooke hesitated. "I don't know," she replied finally. "That's what I'm hoping to find out when I speak to her. I do know that a big block of shares was offered to the conglomerate over the weekend in some sort of a private deal. Fortunately Morgan's bankers heard rumors about the deal in time to warn him, but they didn't know the name of the seller. I want to find out—for personal reasons."

"For personal reasons?" The look Mr. Kent gave Brooke was too shrewd for her comfort. He was silent for a long time, as if considering what he ought to say. "Sheila has a good reason to sell," he said finally. "This takeover bid came at a bad moment for us all, but it was particularly frustrating for Sheila. Last month her fiancé was offered a partnership in an Australian mining venture. They both wanted to accept the offer, but they needed cash—a lot of cash—to buy into the company and to establish themselves in a new home overseas."

"Why doesn't Morgan know about this offer?" Brooke asked. "He had no idea that Sheila wanted to sell her shares."

"David was going to explain the situation and ask Morgan's advice on how best to liquidate Sheila's holding in Kent Industries, but then we learned that the company was threatened by a takeover bid. Sheila realized that she would have to wait before she sold out. I'm wondering if something could have happened to make her change her mind."

"I'm going to call her and find out," Brooke said grimly.

Andy gave a sudden loud cry and they both jumped. The two of them had been so engrossed in their conversation that Andy's activities had passed unnoticed. He and Angela had managed to build an impressive tower of blocks, but the cat, bored with confinement to one room, had taken a sudden flying leap at the tower, sending the pile of blocks tumbling. Andy sobbed noisily as he inspected the ruins of his building project, refusing to let Angela console him.

Brooke found a clean tissue and dried Andy's tears. "Never mind, honey," she said. "We'll go to our room and play with your ball." With the ease of long practice, she balanced her son on one hip and took the slip of paper from Mr. Kent with the other. "Thanks for the phone numbers," she said. "There's a phone in my room, and I'll call New York right now."

"Let me know what happens," Mr. Kent said. "And bring Andy back for another visit this afternoon."

She said good-bye to Angela and her father-in-law and hurried to her room. Her arm was beginning to feel numb by the time she arrived.

"You're getting heavier by the minute, old fellow," she said as she put Andy in his crib. "I think your grandfather must be overfeeding you when he takes you on all those outings."

Andy, who was busily engaged in throwing all his toys out of the crib, didn't bother to reply.

She dialed the number Mr. Kent had given her, but the phone rang unanswered in the apartment where Sheila's fiancé lived. Brooke was about to dial Morgan's investment banking firm, when there was a knock at her door. She opened it to find Sheila standing in the hallway, looking unusually nervous and disheveled.

They stared at one another in silence. "Come in," Brooke said finally, when she had recovered from her surprise. "I've been hoping to talk to you. I was just trying to call you, in fact, when you knocked at the door."

Sheila entered the room and walked jerkily toward Andy's crib. She carefully avoided Brooke's eyes and bent with brittle, nervous movements to pick up the toys he had thrown on the floor. "I just got in from New York," she said. "My father said I had to come and see you. I know why you wanted to find me. You want to talk to me about the shares I sold. My father's very angry with me, and I guess Morgan will be even madder when he finds out what I did."

"Don't you think he has a right to be angry?" Brooke asked. "After all, you did sell him out the moment his back was turned."

"I guess it must seem that way, although that isn't what really happened." Sheila swung away from the crib and looked pleadingly at Brooke.

"Morgan loves you," she said, "and he's got you back now. I thought it wouldn't matter to him so much if he lost control of the company. After all, it isn't as if he's losing his money as well. If the conglomerate decides to buy his personal shareholding, he'll be worth millions."

"Didn't your father tell you? Morgan hasn't lost the company. His brokers intervened on the deal you were arranging with the conglomerate and bought up your shares. Morgan has been able to regain complete control of Kent Industries."

Sheila paled. "I didn't know," she said. "The public announcement must have been made while I was in flight from New York to Boston. And Dad didn't say anything. Maybe he felt I deserved to feel guilty a bit longer." She sank down onto the bed, fumbling inside her purse. "I need a cigarette. Do you mind?" She flicked her lighter and held the flame to her cigarette with an unsteady hand. After a couple of deep inhalations, she gave a little laugh. "So Morgan's still the big boss of Kent Industries. And you know what? I'm not even sure that I'm glad. That company is a monster, eating up our lives, and I think I secretly wanted Morgan to lose control." She inhaled another lungful of smoke, then looked at Brooke. "You probably won't believe this," she said, "but I rationalized the sale of my shares by saying I was doing you a good turn. I told myself I was making up for the problems I caused two years ago. I thought that without Kent Industries to devour his time, Morgan might remember occasionally that he had a wife and son. Now I guess everything is messed up. He still has the company, but I'll bet he mortgaged every damn thing he owns to buy those shares. So he'll be spending more time working away at the office, not less."

"I would think so," Brooke agreed. "Tell me, Sheila, why did you sell those shares at the precise moment you did? Was it something to do with your fiancé and going to Australia?"

"I can see that my father's been talking to you," Sheila said. "You know about David's offer of a partnership?" When Brooke nodded, she sighed and looked round for an ashtray in which to stub out her cigarette. "David got a telephone call on Saturday morning, just after you'd left for the cabin," she said. "The company in Australia found another qualified mining engineer willing to buy into the partnership, and they wanted David's decision right away. Apparently they'd been pressing David for a decision for weeks now, and he just didn't tell me. He felt I had enough worries, what with Andrew's accident and the takeover bid and everything." She looked appealingly at Brooke. "We needed the money desperately, and there was no way we could contact Morgan. In the end I decided that selling my shares would work out better for everybody, even if Morgan did lose control of Kent Industries."

"That was a very convenient conclusion," Brooke said, struggling to control her anger at Sheila's glib explanations. She sighed. "Who knows? Perhaps it will work out all right in the end. You and David will be able to go to Australia, and, as it turns out, Morgan still has his company."

Sheila tossed her blond curls out of her eyes and jumped off the bed. "I'm so glad you're not angry with me," she said. "I knew you'd understand my point of view once I explained what really happened." She hurried on, not giving Brooke a chance to say anything. "I guess I'd better go and have a shower, tidy myself up and all that. I ought to see my father right away and tell him that I've made my confession. And I want to talk to him about the arrangements for my wedding. David and I will have to be married soon."

She smiled brightly, but once again she was careful to avoid Brooke's eyes. "I just have to ask you for one favor, Brooke. Would *you* explain to Morgan why I sold those shares? I'm . . . er . . . sure he must be busy at the office, and I'd rather not disturb him right at the moment."

"I'd much prefer it if you told Morgan the truth yourself," Brooke said. "Besides, don't you think you owe him at least that much?"

Sheila stretched out her hand in an unconscious gesture of appeal. "You know he won't understand why I did it," she said. "And David is waiting for me to join him right now, so that we can discuss the arrangements for our wedding with my father."

"Right now? Is David here, then?"

"Yes, he flew up with me from New York. Brooke, the partners want us to be in Australia by the middle of next month and there's so much to do. I'm relying on you to explain everything to Morgan. I don't want him to blame David for anything, and he'll listen to you without getting angry."

"Do you really believe that?" Brooke asked.

Sheila hurried to the bedroom door. "You know how Morgan feels about you," she said, avoiding a direct answer to Brooke's ironic question. "Well, bye! Like I said, I have to run now. David and I have a *zillion* things to discuss with my father."

She was halfway into the hallway before she finished speaking, and she stuck her head back around the door to complete her good-byes. "Take care, Andy!" she called out. "Stop throwing your toys on the floor or they're going to break!"

Brooke waited until the sound of Sheila's footsteps had faded away, then she turned to Andy with a tiny, rueful smile. "She's quite right about the toys, you know, even if she's all wrong about everything else. You're going to ruin them if you keep doing that."

Andy picked up his teddy bear and his security blanket, which were the only things remaining in his crib. He looked at Brooke over the comforting hump of his blanket. "Go walk," he said firmly, obviously deciding that his mother's remarks didn't merit a reply.

"Okay, we'll go for a walk," she said, "while I decide what I'm going to say to your father." He crowed with delight and gave her a hug, but Brooke's answering smile was strained. "Oh, Andy," she said, as she removed their winter jackets from the closet. "If only your father was as easy to please as you are!"

Chapter Twelve

BROOKE DIDN'T RECOGNIZE THE GIRL in charge of reception, although that wasn't surprising. It had been nearly three years since her last visit to the Kent Industries headquarters in downtown Boston.

"Good evening," she said.

"Good evening." The receptionist acknowledged Brooke's presence with a slight smile and put aside the pile of technical magazines she was tidying. "The offices are about to close for the night," she said. "But is there some way I could help you?"

"I've come to see my husband. I'm Mrs. Kent."

"Oh!" The receptionist was young and she didn't do a very good job of disguising her astonishment. Her first gasp was clearly audible, although she managed to swallow the second. "I'm sorry I didn't recognize you, Mrs. Kent. I didn't know Mr. Kent was still married...er... that is, I'll call his secretary right away so that she can tell him you've arrived."

"He isn't expecting me," Brooke said. "And there's no need to bother his secretary. I can find my own way if his offices are still in the corner suite on this floor."

"Yes, the executive offices are all on this floor." The receptionist cleared her throat awkwardly. "Mr. Kent has been in meetings all day, Mrs. Kent. I believe a conference with the company's investment bankers is still going on."

"Don't worry, I won't interrupt anything."

Brooke walked slowly along the corridor to Morgan's private office suite. She hesitated for a moment outside his door, then knocked once on the thick, oaken panels and went in, not giving herself time for second thoughts.

She found herself in the midst of a throng of soberly clad businessmen. The door to the conference room stood open, but the huge conference table was deserted. The overflowing ashtrays and crumpled sheets of yellow paper attested to the fact that a meeting had taken place. Despite the crush of people in the outer office, Brooke identified Morgan's tall figure immediately. She watched him as he spoke to a group of executives, and compassion stirred in her when she saw the deep lines of exhaustion etched into every part of his face.

She was sure she had made no sound or movement that would indicate her arrival, but Morgan's head turned suddenly, almost as if he had sensed her presence, and his gaze searched the crowded room. He quickly found her, and their eyes locked in an intimate, silent acknowledgment. She saw him murmur something to the men grouped around him before he pushed his way through the crowd to her side.

"This is a surprise," he said without offering any other greeting.

"I hope it's a pleasant one."

"Why have you come?" Although his voice might have sounded normal enough to his business colleagues,

Brooke had no difficulty recognizing the heavy thread of tension that ran through his words.

"Sheila asked me to discuss something with you, and I thought it might be easier in your office." His tension communicated itself to her, and she felt her voice tighten. "I wasn't expecting to find the place quite so crowded."

"The meeting is virtually over," he said. "Everybody will be leaving within five minutes. Half the people in the room have planes to catch, and the other half have been working nonstop the entire day. If you go into my private office, I'll be able to join you very shortly."

She looked at the uncompromising line of his mouth and the rigid set of his shoulders, and her courage began to desert her. "You don't have to finish the meetings on my account. Perhaps it would be better if we talked later."

"No," he said sharply. "We need to talk now." His body stiffened as he spoke, and she realized with a jolt of amazement that he was even more uptight than she was. He turned abruptly away from her. "I'll only be a minute," he repeated.

She didn't know how to start their discussion when he joined her in his office, closing the door firmly behind him. She had rehearsed her speech a dozen times during the afternoon, but now the carefully prepared words fled, leaving her mind blank and her body trembling with awareness of Morgan's nearness.

"Everybody's gone," he said. "Even my secretary. We won't be disturbed. There's nobody left in this part of the building except us and the security guards."

Once again she tried to remember the opening of her prepared speech, but it was hopeless. "How did your meetings go?" she asked, relieved that she had found something more or less sensible to say. "Were they successful?"

"I guess so." His voice was touched with a trace of impatience. "I want to talk about last night," he said. "Brooke, about what happened . . . you were absolutely right to be angry with me. As soon as Angela mentioned that those shares had been offered for sale, I jumped to the conclusion that you'd taken me up to the cabin in order to keep me out of reach of a telephone. It was an irrational conclusion, and I behaved very badly."

His apology was so unexpected that for a moment she could only stare at him in silence. She tried to think of a graceful reply, but her mind remained an infuriating blank. "I didn't sell those shares," she finally blurted out. "Sheila did. She asked me to come here and explain everything to you."

"I know it was Sheila," Morgan replied. "Last night I was too angry to think clearly. I was so afraid that all the plans I'd been making for us were nothing more than castles in the air and that you'd intended all along to leave me. But this morning, thank God, I was functioning a little more rationally. Once I decided to trust you and accept your word that you hadn't sold the shares, it was easy to find out who was responsible. It only took me a couple of phone calls to discover that it was Sheila who made the sale."

"I see." Brooke was staring at her hands, and when she saw how tightly clenched they were she made a conscious effort to relax them. Hope started to grow inside her, rushing along her veins and making her shiver with feverish anticipation. She did her best to crush the hope, afraid to ask Morgan exactly what he meant. Could he possibly be saying that he cared deeply about giving their marriage another chance? Was he telling her that he had behaved irrationally because he had felt hurt by her supposed betrayal? She cleared her throat nervously. "Sheila asked me to explain to you why she sold the shares, Morgan. She didn't mean to act behind your back, but she needed the money in a hurry...."

Morgan interrupted her, swearing long and fluently under his breath. "At this precise moment, I don't give a damn about Sheila and her motives." He looked searchingly at Brooke, and a trace of color darkened the austere line of his cheekbones. "I only care about you," he said.

His gaze seemed fixed on a stack of files, so he didn't see her eyes blaze with the sudden flare of emotion that she could no longer conceal. He walked stiffly across the room to the window and parted the venetian blinds, staring out through the cracks to the Boston city lights gleaming below. "I did quite a bit of thinking this morning," he said. "I thought about the things you said to me last night, and I decided it was high time for me to reevaluate the priorities in my life. So this morning I called a special board meeting and informed my investment bankers and the senior executives of Kent Industries that I'm planning to sell half my shares to the conglomerate."

"You're planning *what!*" Brooke jumped out of her chair, shaking her head in bewilderment. "I know I can't have understood you. I thought I heard you say that you're planning to sell some of your own shares to the conglomerate. Haven't you spent the last month fighting desperately to prevent people from doing just that?"

"I've changed my strategy," he said curtly. "I've now decided to sell half of my shares."

"But what about all the people who work for you? Won't they be in danger of losing their jobs if you sell out?"

"I intend to offer the directors of the conglomerate some sort of joint-venture agreement. Since I currently control a majority of the shares, I think I can negotiate from a position of strength. At the very worst, I should be able to protect people's jobs long enough for them to look around for other employment. Fortunately all the workers in this company are highly skilled, and even if the conglomerate wants to make changes, my employees shouldn't have much difficulty finding other jobs. Thank God I'm not president of a steel mill, or I'd never be able to strike a bargain."

She drew in a deep, ragged breath. "I'm still not sure that I've understood exactly what this sale will entail. Are you planning to step down from the presidency of Kent Industries?"

The silence stretched out endlessly. "I would prefer to remain president," he said at last. "Kent Industries is a profitable corporation, and I believe I've done a good job running the company. But in selling my controlling interest to the conglomerate, I have to accept the fact that they may prefer to install their own man in the job."

"Why are you doing this, Morgan? Kent Industries has always been the most important thing in your life. Why give it up?"

He turned around from the window at last, and his face seemed gray in the harshness of the fluorescent strip lighting. "I used to think Kent Industries was my life," he said quietly. "But I've found out over the past two years that there are lots of other things that are more important to me."

She walked slowly across to his side, no longer attempting to hold down the fierce blaze of hope that flooded through her. "What things?" she said. "Please tell me, Morgan."

He was silent for so long that she thought he was going to refuse to answer her. When he began speaking, the words seemed almost dragged from him. "When we first got married, I was afraid to admit to myself how important you were to me. If you love somebody very much, you leave yourself intensely vulnerable. I'd never felt that way before, and I didn't want to be hurt, so I did my best to deny my own feelings."

"And now?" she asked softly.

"Now it's too late for pride, and much too late to

worry about feeling vulnerable. Two years ago, after you'd left me, I used to fantasize about how I would punish you once I found you again. I wanted to see you suffer every bit as much as I had. Can you imagine what I felt like when you sent those flowers and I knew that at last I was going to be able to track you down?"

"From the way you behaved," Brooke said, "it's not at all difficult to believe you were planning how best to punish me."

"I was so tense I could scarcely speak when I saw you walking toward me across the lobby of Tony's Bar. I couldn't make up my mind whether I wanted to grab you and shake you senseless or whether I wanted to throw you into the nearest bed and make love to you until we both dropped from exhaustion." His mouth twisted into a faint, wry smile. "You know which fantasy won out," he said.

"Do you know what my fantasy used to be?" she said. "Would you like to hear it?"

Morgan nodded.

"I imagined us living in our own home, with our handsome son and our beautiful daughter. You came home every night in time for an early dinner, and I worked two or three days a week at Boston's finest art gallery. In my dreams you were the sort of husband who always had time to take me out to dinner and to plan wonderful family vacations for our perfectly behaved children."

Morgan's face turned pale. "That's why I'm selling my shares," he said. He drew in a deep breath, as if in preparation for swallowing a large glass of unpleasant medicine. "If the conglomerate agrees to a joint venture, I'll have plenty of time to be the sort of husband you want me to be." He hesitated before adding gruffly, "I love you, Brooke, more than I've ever told you, and I want to please you."

Brooke reached up and touched him very gently on

his cheek. "And I love you, Morgan. I'm overwhelmed at how much you're prepared to sacrifice for my sake. But although I truly appreciate your offer, I don't want you to sell your shares."

"Not sell them? Brooke, I don't understand."

"Don't you see, Morgan? What I described to you was just . . . a dream. I love *you*, the man you really are. Why should you try to change yourself into a totally different person? I chose to marry Morgan Kent, the president of Kent Industries. You don't need to conform to some teenage fantasy of mine that I might not even like if it were translated into reality. Your intelligence and your ambition are an essential part of the man I love. It's taken me a long time to realize that, Morgan, but I've learned to understand my own feelings at last."

He took her into his arms, holding her tightly and lowering his lips to cover her mouth with a burning kiss. "I love you more than anything in this world," he murmured against her mouth. "I would willingly sell everything I possess if that's what I have to do in order to keep you by my side for the rest of our lives."

Her breath quickened with a surge of love, and she smiled teasingly at him. "I'll keep that in mind if I ever decide that I want to be the wife of an idle, layabout millionaire!"

"What about you?" he asked, still holding her within the circle of his arms. His hand stroked her wrist, warm against her skin, and she struggled to concentrate on what he was saying. "Do you want to look for a job in a museum or an art gallery? Something that would make use of your special skills?"

"Yes, of course I do—eventually. But right now I'm happy to spend some time at home with Andy. You're a lucky man, Morgan! Eighteen months of working at Tony's Bar has helped to domesticate me. I can see all sorts of advantages to being a full-time homemaker that I never saw before!"

His hand moved from her wrist and began to caress the delicate skin at her throat. "In that case, time seems to be on my side," he said. "You may as well know right now that there's one part of your fantasy I can't wait to bring true."

"What's that?" she asked.

"The beautiful, well-behaved baby daughter. Do you remember mentioning her? We did such an excellent job of producing a son, I think we ought to set to work right away on producing the missing member of our dream family."

"Right now?" she said. "Here in your office?"

"As a dynamic, resourceful executive," he said, "I'm prepared for any eventuality. As you can see, my office is appointed with a fine leather couch."

She looked at him, faintly startled, and the laughter faded from his eyes to be replaced by a fierce, tender yearning.

"I love you, Brooke," he said. "Will you love me now?"

His kiss swept all logical protest from her mind, as she felt her body yield to the passionate demands of his mouth. He took her hand and guided it inside his shirt, so that she felt the hard smoothness of his rib cage and the accelerated rhythm of his heartbeat. She sighed with pleasure as he undressed her, returning his kisses with a hunger that left both of them shivering with desire.

He swung her up into his arms, and within seconds she felt the coolness of the soft leather cushions against her back and the warmth of Morgan's body on top of hers. The couch, the office, and the world disappeared as she drowned herself in the flood of Morgan's loving.

Long afterward they rested drowsily in each other's arms, whispering tender words of love. It was a long time before Morgan raised himself on one arm and dropped delicate kisses on her eyelids. "It's time to go home," he said softly. "Are you ready, my darling?"

She smiled at him, her love warming her eyes. "Yes, I'm ready, Morgan," she said. "Please take me home."

Second Chance at Love

All of the above titles are $1.75 per copy

Second Chance at Love

All of the above titles are $1.75 per copy

Available at your local bookstore or return this form to:

SECOND CHANCE AT LOVE
The Berkley/Jove Publishing Group
200 Madison Avenue, New York, New York 10016

Please enclose 75¢ for postage and handling for one book, 25¢ each add'l. book ($1.50 max.). No cash, CODs or stamps. Total amount enclosed: $ _____ in check or money order.

NAME _____

ADDRESS _____

CITY_____ STATE/ZIP _____

Allow six weeks for delivery.

WHAT READERS SAY ABOUT SECOND CHANCE AT LOVE

"SECOND CHANCE AT LOVE is fantastic."
—*J. L., Greenville, South Carolina**

"SECOND CHANCE AT LOVE has all the romance of the big novels."
—*L. W., Oak Grove, Missouri**

"You deserve a standing ovation!"
—*S. C., Birch Run, Michigan**

"Thank you for putting out this type of story. Love and passion have no time limits. I look forward to more of these good books."
—*E. G., Huntsville, Alabama**

"Thank you for your excellent series of books. Our book stores receive their monthly selections between the second and third week of every month. Please believe me when I say they have a frantic female calling them every day until they get your books in."
—*C. Y., Sacramento, California**

"I have become addicted to the SECOND CHANCE AT LOVE books...You can be very proud of these books....I look forward to them each month."
—*D. A., Floral City, Florida**

"I have enjoyed every one of your SECOND CHANCE AT LOVE books. Reading them is like eating potato chips, once you start you just can't stop."
—*L. S., Kenosha, Wisconsin**

"I consider your SECOND CHANCE AT LOVE books the best on the market."
—*D. S., Redmond, Washington**

*Names and addresses available upon request